To Binky, Howdy, Tuppy,
and apartment pets everywhere

—E. E.

THE GREAT PET HEIST

Emily Ecton

art by David Mottram

Atheneum Books for Young Readers

New York   London   Toronto   Sydney   New Delhi

$\mathcal{A}$
atheneum

ATHENEUM BOOKS FOR YOUNG READERS

An imprint of Simon & Schuster Children's Publishing Division

1230 Avenue of the Americas, New York, New York 10020

ATHENEUM BOOKS FOR YOUNG READERS is a registered trademark of
Simon & Schuster, Inc. Atheneum logo is a trademark of Simon & Schuster, Inc.

For information about special discounts for bulk purchases, please contact Simon &
Schuster Special Sales at 1-866-506-1949 or business@simonandschuster.com.

The Simon & Schuster Speakers Bureau can bring authors to your live event.

For more information or to book an event, contact the Simon & Schuster
Speakers Bureau at 1-866-248-3049 or visit our website at www.simonspeakers.com.

Also available in an Atheneum Books for Young Readers hardcover edition

Interior design by Tom Daly

The text for this book was set in Excelsior LT Std.

The illustrations for this book were rendered digitally.

Manufactured in the United States of America

0821 MTN

First Atheneum Books for Young Readers paperback edition May 2021

4 6 8 10 9 7 5

The Library of Congress has cataloged the hardcover edition as follows:

Names: Ecton, Emily, author. | Mottram, Dave, illustrator.

Title: The great pet heist / Emily Ecton ; illustrated by Dave Mottram.

Description: First edition. | New York City : Atheneum Books for Young Readers, [2020] |
Audience: Ages 8–12. | Audience: Grades 4–6. | Summary: When their elderly owner goes
to the hospital, Butterbean the dachshund, Walt the cat, Oscar the mynah bird,
and rats Marco and Polo plan a robbery to support themselves.

Identifiers: LCCN 2019035648 | ISBN 9781534455368 (hardcover) |
ISBN 9781534455375 (pbk) | ISBN 9781534455382 (eBook)

Subjects: CYAC: Pets—Fiction. | Robbers and outlaws—Fiction. | Humorous stories.

Classification: LCC PZ7.E21285 Gre 2020 | DDC [Fic]—dc23

LC record available at https://lccn.loc.gov/2019035648

— 1 —

BUTTERBEAN KNEW SHE WASN'T ALWAYS A GOOD dog. But until the morning of Tuesday, October 20, she'd never considered herself a BAD dog. And she definitely never thought that by Wednesday, October 21, she'd be a member of an International Crime Syndicate.

"The Fall," as they all described it afterward, happened at precisely 10 a.m. (Oscar was watching the clock. His shows were coming on.)

The tile in the kitchen had always been a little slippery, but on Tuesday, October 20, it was much more slippery than usual, mostly because Butterbean had just thrown up on it.

To be fair, she'd spent most of the morning chasing her tail, and she'd actually been feeling pretty proud of herself for barfing on the tile instead of the cream-colored carpet.

But that was before everything changed.

At precisely 9:59 a.m. Central Time (one minute before *The Price Is Right*), Mrs. Food emerged from her office and started down the hallway for her second cup of coffee. Exactly forty-five seconds later, her foot made contact with Butterbean's former breakfast. And at 10 a.m. on the dot, she hit the floor.

The crash was so loud and it scared Butterbean so badly that she tried to wedge herself into the gap under the couch. (She was not successful.)

It was so loud that Walt stopped her morning grooming ritual and sat frozen for a full minute with her tongue out and her leg poised in midair.

It was so loud that Oscar squawked and puffed his feathers out in a very undignified way. (Oscar denies this.)

Then there was a terrible silence.

No one moved.

Finally Walt lowered her leg and glared at Butterbean. "Way to go, Pukey."

Butterbean ignored the comment. It was hardly her fault that Mrs. Food had decided to take a nap.

It wasn't even unusual for Mrs. Food to lie down—
she did that all the time. Sure, she usually did it on
the couch or on her bed or someplace squishy. But
Butterbean wasn't one to judge.

Butterbean did wish that Mrs. Food would get up,
though. Butterbean had never seen her lie on the floor
quite like that. It seemed wrong, somehow.

"Mrs. Food?" Butterbean said.

Mrs. Food didn't respond.

Butterbean frowned.

Usually Mrs. Food got cranky when Butterbean tried
to chat during her naptime. Sometimes she even threw
pillows or socks, which was huge fun. But this time she
just lay there. She didn't even look comfortable.

A terrible thought crossed Butterbean's mind.

Maybe this wasn't a nap.

"Mrs. Food?" Butterbean said again, but louder.
"Are you dead?"

Still nothing from Mrs. Food.

"Is that a yes?" Butterbean said after what she
thought was an appropriate amount of time. She
wasn't sure how long dead people usually took to
respond. She was willing to be patient.

"Check her vitals," Oscar said from his cage overhead.

"Yes. Her vitals. Of course." Butterbean went

cautiously over to Mrs. Food and began inspecting her carefully, starting with the butt. "Where would those be, exactly?"

Walt snorted from the top of the bookshelf. Which was not particularly helpful, in Butterbean's opinion.

Oscar fluffed his feathers in irritation. The shows he watched made it very clear that the vitals were important, but unfortunately, they weren't very clear about the specifics. Like location, for instance. Not that he wanted to admit that. He was obviously a very well-informed bird, and well-informed birds knew about things like vitals.

"In her mouth," he said after a moment. He was pretty sure that was right. And it wasn't like Butterbean would know either way.

"Got it." Butterbean stuck her nose as close to Mrs. Food's mouth as physically possible. "Her vitals smell like . . . coffee and . . . something minty. Is that good?"

Oscar hesitated. He'd never heard anyone on his doctor shows use the word "minty" to describe vitals. Minty only came up in the commercials, but it was generally positive. That must be good, then. Oscar nodded confidently. "Yes, minty sounds good. Now wake her up."

Butterbean nodded. Obviously this was not a situation where low woofs and intense staring would do the job. This situation called for more drastic measures. Serious stuff. The Big Guns. It was time for licking up the nostril.

Butterbean got herself into prime nostril-licking position. She was just deciding which nostril to try first when Walt jumped down from her bookshelf and pushed Butterbean aside.

"Oh no you don't." Walt sat on Mrs. Food's chest, tail twitching. "We don't have time for a nostril probe."

Butterbean blinked. There was ALWAYS time for a nostril probe.

Walt raised a paw and soundly bopped Mrs. Food on the nose. "Hey! HEY!" She bopped three more times in rapid succession and then shook her head. "No good. She's out cold."

Oscar sighed. "Well, we've done all we can."

"Now the nostril probe?" Butterbean said hopefully.

Oscar shook his head sadly. "If Walt's paw bop didn't do it, nothing will, I'm afraid. It's hopeless."

Walt narrowed her eyes. "Not quite. We could use the secret device."

Butterbean gasped.

"You wouldn't dare!" Oscar screeched.

The secret device was a small plastic box with a button that Mrs. Food wore on a cord around her neck. She always said that if anything happened to her, the device would save her. (Although from what Butterbean could tell, it hadn't done much so far in the way of saving.) What the device *was* had been the subject of much debate. Oscar maintained that they didn't need to know what it was, and Walt just wanted to push the button. Because, you know, buttons.

"WE DON'T EVEN KNOW WHAT THE DEVICE DOES!" Oscar screeched again, raking his beak against the bars of his cage.

Walt just watched him, calmly twitching her tail.

"We don't know what it does," Oscar said, visibly trying to calm himself. "I've seen shows on the Television. It could destroy us all."

"Destroy us all," Butterbean echoed.

"It could mean the end of the world," Oscar said ominously.

"End of the world," Butterbean echoed.

"Of course," Walt said, batting the box with her paw.

"We'll figure out another way," Oscar said. "Right?"

"Right," Butterbean said.

"Right. Of course. We shouldn't push it," Walt said, pushing the button. "Oops, too late."

"WHAT HAVE YOU DONE!" Oscar shrieked, flinging his wing over his face to protect himself, as Butterbean dove for cover under the couch (unsuccessfully again).

There was silence.

"Apparently nothing? Nothing is what it does?" Walt said, swatting the button again. "It's a button that does nothing. Mrs. Food must've been making a joke this whole time."

"It's not a funny joke," Butterbean said, backing away from the couch. She was starting to get a bald spot on the top of her nose from jamming it under the couch so many times. "Not funny ha-ha, anyway."

Although to be fair, sometimes Butterbean didn't get Mrs. Food's sense of humor. She'd never been a fan of the hilarious "we're going for a fun ride, oh wait, it's actually a trip to the vet" joke that Mrs. Food seemed so fond of.

"We're just lucky we weren't blown to smithereens," Oscar said smugly. "We could've all been killed. We need a new house rule about button pushing."

Walt licked her paw and shrugged. "I pushed a button. Sue me. No harm done, right?"

It was then that they heard the sirens.

– 2 –

"WELL, THAT DOESN'T SOUND GOOD," SAID WALT, looking uncertain for the first time.

Then the doors burst open, and the apartment was under attack.

From her position under the coffee table, Butterbean watched three strangers storm the apartment. They were wearing matching outfits and seemed to be aided in their invasion by Bob the maintenance guy. Butterbean growled. Traitor.

"INVADERS! INVADERS!" Oscar shrieked, jumping from his perch to the bottom of his cage in the noisiest way possible. The cage rocked so violently that it sounded like it was about to crash to the floor.

Walt leaped into position on top of the bookshelf and hissed angrily at the strangers, who seemed to have taken an unusual interest in Mrs. Food.

"One wrong move and I'm going for the eyes," Walt said, claws at the ready. She also inadvertently knocked a book off the shelf, but she shot it a look that told it not to try any more funny business. It didn't.

The strangers didn't seem to be intimidated by the fearsome displays put on by Oscar and Walt. (Butterbean wasn't sure if her growls actually qualified as fearsome, but she was doing her best.) In fact, they ignored the animals completely and continued their inspection of Mrs. Food. If Butterbean hadn't known better, she would've said that those were the same checks she and Oscar had tried to do. But slightly more effectively, since they had people hands with working thumbs and seemed to know what they were doing.

"Are they going for her vitals?" Butterbean said. She glared at Bob the maintenance guy. She would deal with him later. Nobody betrayed Mrs. Food and got away with it. Not on Butterbean's watch.

"If they try anything with her vitals, I'm going for the eyes," Walt hissed.

"Are they waking her up? What are they doing!" Oscar screeched angrily. Walt kept waving her tail and blocking his view, so he was missing a good portion of the action. It was very frustrating.

"They're not even going to TRY the deep nostril probe?" Butterbean said, watching carefully. "It's the number one wake-up method!"

"If they try a nostril probe, I'm going for the eyes," Walt hissed again, leaning forward and teetering dangerously on her toes. "We've got to save Mrs. Food."

"Don't go for the eyes, Walt!" Oscar said, hopping onto the side of his cage. "It's too late for Mrs. Food! Save yourselves!"

It looked like Oscar was right. The three strangers grabbed Mrs. Food, and before anyone could launch a counterattack, they loaded her onto a wheely contraption and rolled her out into the hallway. (It was a stretcher, Oscar reminded them later. How could they not remember that? They'd seen them on the Television a thousand times.) At the last minute, Walt tried to go for the eyes, and a panicked Butterbean made a dash for the hallway, but it was no use.

Bob the maintenance guy pushed Butterbean back into the living room with his foot. "Don't worry, dog. Your mommy is in good hands," he said, closing the door behind him.

"Wait, what?" Butterbean said, frowning.

"Don't listen to him. He's delusional," Walt said.

She looked up at Oscar. "Well, now what?" She sat down in front of the door and twitched her tail anxiously.

"We're doomed," Oscar said, sitting on the floor of his cage. He didn't even make sure he was in a clean patch, that's how depressed he was. (He wasn't, incidentally. In a clean patch, that is.)

"Wait, WHAT?" Butterbean gasped. "Mrs. Food is my MOMMY?" She swayed slightly on her feet. It was a lot to take in. She always knew she had a bond with Mrs. Food, sure, but she thought it was more of a snack-based relationship.

"Good grief," Walt muttered under her breath. "Not this again. Oscar?"

Oscar sighed. "No, Butterbean, Mrs. Food is not your mommy. We've been over this before. You were adopted, just like the rest of us," he said, still sitting on the floor of his cage.

"There are papers," Walt said. "I've seen them."

"Ah. Papers." Butterbean nodded in relief. She did remember having this talk before, but she still didn't understand why people like Bob kept lying to her about her relationship with Mrs. Food. It was very confusing.

Walt rolled her eyes and turned back to the door. All three animals watched it carefully. It didn't open.

"So what now?" Butterbean said. Her butt had started to go numb from sitting so long.

"What do you mean, what now?" Oscar said. Only the top of his head was visible from Butterbean's position on the floor. It was a little disturbing to Butterbean that he hadn't gotten back up onto his perch.

"I mean, what do we do now? How long until Mrs. Food comes back? I miss her."

"We do nothing now. There's nothing to do. Mrs. Food isn't coming back. Ever. We're doomed." Oscar's voice was totally flat. Butterbean had never heard him sound that way before. His voice usually fell somewhere between shrill and shrieky. If she didn't know better, she'd say he sounded depressed.

"What? But I want Mrs. Food back," Butterbean whimpered.

"Me too," Walt said under her breath.

"It doesn't matter. She's gone." Oscar didn't even look up.

"But Bob said not to worry."

"Bob's a liar," Walt said.

"Bob said Mrs. Food is your MOMMY," Oscar said.

Butterbean winced. "Yes. I remember that." She licked her lips anxiously. "But who will feed us? I can't use the can opener. And who will take me out? Will I use Walt's box?" Butterbean tried to control the panic in her voice, but it was hard. She was starting to freak out.

"You're not using my box." Walt shot her a nasty look.

"NO ONE!" Oscar screeched finally, jumping up onto his perch. "No one is walking you. Don't you get it? Mrs. Food is gone. I've seen this on the Television.

When people go out in stretchers, they don't come back. And as for food, even if we could open the cans, we're still doomed, because we can't get new ones. According to my sources, a can of dog food costs a dollar forty-five. And I don't have that kind of money. Do you?"

Butterbean shook her head. That sounded like a lot.

"Sources? What sources?" Walt asked skeptically.

"THE PRICE IS RIGHT!" Oscar screeched. "My Television sources are never wrong! Grocery products are very expensive!"

Butterbean nodded in agreement. She wasn't as into *The Price Is Right* as Oscar was, so she wasn't entirely sure of her facts. But she definitely didn't have a dollar forty-five. "But wait. You mean Mrs. Food is gone forever? She won't be walking me ever again?"

"Yes. Gone. Forever." Oscar tucked his head under his wing, ending the conversation.

Butterbean looked at Walt, who shrugged and went back to watching the door.

Butterbean lay her head on her paws and watched too. Just in case Mrs. Food came back.

They were still watching as the light faded and the room grew darker.

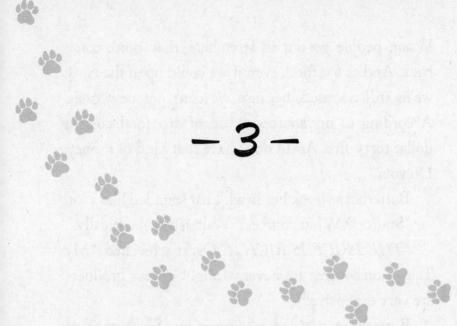

– 3 –

WHEN THE KEY TURNED IN THE LOCK,
Butterbean jumped to her feet. She wasn't sure how
much time had passed, but she had definitely been
awake the whole time and hadn't fallen asleep once.
Not even when she'd rested her eyes that one time.
Okay, two times.

"Heads up," Walt whispered. "Stranger danger."

Butterbean sniffed nervously. Walt was right. It
wasn't Mrs. Food coming through that door, that
was for sure. Whoever was coming in smelled more
like erasers and pencils and fruit juice and pretzels.
Butterbean hadn't ever smelled that particular combi-
nation before—she'd remember someone who smelled

like pretzels. "Any ideas?" Butterbean whispered to Walt.

Walt shook her head. "Be ready for anything."

Butterbean sniffed again and felt the fur stand up on the back of her neck. She recognized a new smell. It was the smell of spackle and paint and toilet cleaner. Butterbean felt a growl form in the back of her throat. She knew who that was. BOB.

"Easy, Bean," Walt whispered again. "Wait till the door opens. Then you go for the ankles. I'll handle the rest."

"Got it," Butterbean said, swallowing her growl. She really wanted to let loose with the barks, but she knew the element of surprise was important. She'd learned that much from Oscar's shows.

The door swung open, revealing two people silhouetted in the doorway.

"Now!" Walt said. "Wha— Abort! Abort!" Her pounce turned into an awkward hop.

"Walt." Butterbean stopped with one foot in the air, then overbalanced and landed in a clumsy heap. "That's a kid. Do I go for the ankles on a kid? That doesn't seem right."

"Hold your position," Walt said. "We need to reassess."

Standing in front of Bob in the doorway was a

medium-sized girl, not a baby, but also not a grown-up. She had long straight black hair, and she gave a little wave when she spotted Butterbean and Walt.

Butterbean blinked. She'd never been waved to before.

Walt narrowed her eyes in suspicion. It was obviously a tactical maneuver designed to make them let down their guard. But Walt was onto her. It wouldn't work.

"So here they all are," Bob said, flipping on the lights without even giving the animals a heads-up so they could shield their eyes. Walt hissed. Oscar gave

a bloodcurdling scream, followed by some low-level grumbling.

Bob pointed at Butterbean.

"That's the dog, there. It's the biggest problem."

"Thanks," Butterbean muttered.

Bob acted like she hadn't even said anything. "It'll need to be walked what—two, three times a day maybe? I don't know, however many times dogs need to be walked so they don't mess up the carpet."

"Ten," Butterbean said seriously. "I need to go outside ten times a day. Maybe twenty."

"Shut it, Butterbean," Walt hissed. "Don't engage with them."

"Okay, so I'll walk her three times a day. What's her name?" the girl asked, squatting down to look at Butterbean.

"Says here . . ." Bob consulted a crumpled piece of paper in his hand. "Oscar. No, that's the bird. The dog is Butterbean. He's a wiener dog."

"She," Butterbean corrected. "I'm a she. SHE'S a wiener dog."

The girl stroked Butterbean's ear. "Long hair for a wiener dog."

"I'm a long-haired wiener dog," Butterbean said. She didn't know whether this girl could be trusted, but she did appreciate a good ear rub.

"Mouthy little mutt," Bob said, giving Butterbean a dismissive look. He wasn't a dog person. "So that's the dog. And that up there, that's the bird. Oscar. It's a mynah bird, so don't be freaked out if it talks to you. According to this it can say words."

"Kiss off," Oscar said in his best out-loud Human voice. He was in no mood. He glared at the girl almost like they were in a staring contest.

"Boy, you're not kidding," the girl said, her eyes wide.

Bob didn't seem to notice. "You don't need to do much there, just change the food and water and paper, if it gets gross. And that down there is Lucretia."

Butterbean cocked her head. "Who's Lucretia?"

The girl broke eye contact with Oscar (who silently cheered himself for winning the staring contest) and looked back at Bob. "Which one is Lucretia?"

Bob pointed at Walt. "That one. That weird-looking black cat with the long nose."

"I'm an Oriental shorthair, thank you," Walt said quietly. "And my name is Walt."

"Huh." The girl squatted down next to Walt and stared into her eyes. "You don't look like a Lucretia to me," she said.

"I'm not. My name is Walt," Walt said.

"You look more like a . . . hmm . . ." The girl cocked

her head in almost the same way Butterbean had. "What do you look like?"

"Walt," Walt said. "I look like Walt."

"You look more like . . ."

"Walt," Butterbean barked.

"Walt," Walt said again.

"You look more like a . . . Walt."

"I like this girl," Walt said, turning to Butterbean. "The attack is canceled."

"How'd you DO that?" Butterbean stared at Walt in amazement.

Walt shrugged.

Bob snorted. "Look, kid, I don't care what you call them, as long as you take care of them, okay? It's not like they'll be around long, if you know what I mean."

The animals got very still.

"What do you mean?" the girl asked.

"Just between us, it doesn't look like their owner is going to be coming back any time soon. Don't get too attached or you're in for heartache."

"But why?" the girl said.

"Look, she's got no family, okay? Even if she gets better, she's probably heading for a home, and these guys? Well, nobody wants to take care of a pack of stinking animals. If it was just one, maybe, but this gang? I'd say they have a week, more or less."

"A week?"

"Give or take. Then it's the pound for them. It's not like they can take care of themselves. So like I said. Don't get attached."

"Right." The girl looked doubtful. "Me, I can take care of myself."

Bob gave her a strange look. "That's great, kid. Now maybe you should stop with the jaw flapping and walk this guy?"

"Girl," Butterbean pouted.

Bob consulted the list. "Hold off just a minute. I almost forgot the last two."

He disappeared into Mrs. Food's office.

"Last two?" Butterbean cocked her head again. It was getting quite a workout.

"Clear a space on the table, okay, kid?" Bob called from the office.

"Sure." The girl looked almost as confused as Butterbean, but she cleared away Mrs. Food's newspaper and place mats.

"Whoooaaa whooooaaaa!!!"

She had hardly cleared a space when she was stopped short by series of shrieks coming from the office. Tiny, thin shrieks that sounded like someone very small riding a roller coaster. Or two someones.

Bob came in carrying a glass aquarium. The shrieks

got louder. They were definitely coming from inside the aquarium.

"Whooooaaa whoooaaa WHOOOOAAAA!! YEE-HAW!!" came a tiny voice.

"AIIIIEEEE! MAKE IT STOP!!" came another tiny voice.

Butterbean stared at the aquarium in horror. There were two rats inside, and they weren't even attempting to hide. One was covering its face with its paws and peeking out through its fingers as it tried to keep its balance. The other was waving its arms in the air and shrieking with glee, like the moving aquarium was a surfboard or a Tilt-A-Whirl.

"WHO ARE THEY??" Butterbean squealed, trying to get a closer look.

"Down, boy," Bob said, nudging Butterbean aside.

Butterbean toppled onto her back in shock, furious at herself. She had often thought, while she chewed on her rawhide chew or disemboweled a squeaky vegetable, that Mrs. Food's office smelled like it might have an infestation of some sort. There had been some distinctly ratty odors wafting through the doorway occasionally. Not all the time, but often enough. But then she would realize how unlikely that was, laugh quietly to herself, and go back to her chew toy. Because come on. Mrs. Food's OFFICE?

Infested with RATS? Hardy-har-har. And yet, here was Bob with the cold hard evidence. Butterbean's whole life was a lie.

"So yeah, these two also. I guess just keep their cage from stinking and give them food and whatever. Looks like they're good on water, but keep an eye out."

The girl peered inside the aquarium. The rats stared back at her. They'd stopped acting like they were on their own personal amusement park ride and were watching her expectantly. "Do they have names?"

Bob checked the crumpled paper in his hand. "They didn't give me names. So just Rat One and Rat Two, I guess. Or call that one Colleen and that one Elizabeth. Who cares? I mean, they're rats. It's not like they know the difference."

"HEY!" said one of the rats (aka Colleen).

"RUDE," said the other one (aka Elizabeth).

Butterbean slowly turned from the infestation and stared at Walt in horror. Walt, who spent a good amount of time in the office. Walt, who could climb on high surfaces. Walt, who liked to keep secrets.

"Did you KNOW?" Butterbean demanded. "That we had RATS?"

Walt shrugged.

"You KNEW? And you didn't say ANYTHING?"

Walt shrugged again. "I didn't know it was a secret.

They were right there on the shelf. You went in the office. They weren't hidden."

Butterbean's jaw dropped. "I'm SHORT. I'm a SHORT DOG. I don't see things up high. YOU KNOW THAT."

"Well, I'm sorry. I'm telling you now. We've got rats."

"Yes, so I understand. Rat One and Rat Two," Butterbean grumbled. "And those are just the ones we can SEE."

"Marco!"

"Polo!"

Butterbean whipped her head around and glared at the aquarium. "EXCUSE ME?"

"I'm Marco," said Rat One (aka Colleen).

"And I'm Polo," said Rat Two (aka Elizabeth).

"We don't really go by Rat One and Rat Two, no matter what that guy says."

"Or Colleen and Elizabeth. That guy is bonkers."

"Totally." Marco rolled his eyes.

"Totally," Polo echoed, making twirly "crazy" motions next to her head.

"Well, yeah." Butterbean had to agree there. They may be infesting the office, but those rats weren't stupid.

"Ahem."

The animals immediately stopped their conversation and stared up at the girl, who was looking at them with a puzzled expression. "Are they always this . . . chatty?"

Bob shrugged and handed her Butterbean's leash. "How would I know? Mice squeak, right? They're chatty. Dogs too, I guess."

"Rats," Marco and Polo said in unison. "Not mice."

"Right." The girl frowned. She clipped the leash onto Butterbean's collar.

"Bean," Oscar said in a low voice. "Be careful. Observe everything. Urgent house meeting when you return."

"Okay," Butterbean said, trying hard to control her tail. It was her natural instinct to start wagging when the leash went on, but it didn't seem appropriate this time, somehow.

"House meeting," she said as she trotted to the door, girl in tow. "Urgent meeting. Got it."

"Urgent," Oscar said as the door shut behind them. "Because if what Bob just said is true, I was right. We're all in serious trouble."

– 4 –

BUTTERBEAN WAS DOING HER JAUNTY WALK WHEN she came back. Tail wagging, high bouncing, the whole bit. Oscar was disgusted.

Butterbean obviously didn't understand how serious their situation was. Oscar averted his eyes as Butterbean licked the girl on the hand and then bounced on into the living room.

"Hoo! What a workout!" Butterbean flopped down onto the carpet as the girl left the apartment. Oscar gave her a disapproving look, but she didn't seem to notice.

"That girl goes so much faster than Mrs. Food! My legs were flying!" Butterbean went on, tongue lolling out of her mouth.

Oscar cleared his throat. "Yes, well, obviously. Mrs. Food was older, and susceptible to falls. I'm surprised you didn't realize that. Especially in light of recent events."

"Right. Falls." Butterbean snuffled in embarrassment. "Look, I SAID I was SORRY, okay?" She wished she hadn't said anything. She was never going to live that barf down.

Walt put a paw on Butterbean's back. "It's fine. Now, what happened while you were out there? Did you see or hear anything? Do you have any new information?"

Butterbean looked at the ceiling while she thought. It was important to focus so she wouldn't forget anything. She didn't want to mess this up too. "Yeeess. There was something. They're using a new cleaner on the rugs—it's very strong. I think it's supposed to be a floral smell? I don't like it."

Oscar raised an eyebrow at Walt. "Okay, that's new. And?"

"I saw Biscuit from the second floor. He has a new haircut. You can see his eyes again. It's a good look."

Walt refused to even glance at Oscar. "And?"

Butterbean considered for a minute. "Well . . . there's been a lot of activity at the trash can out front. Mostly Biscuit, I think, but I think someone new had been by too. OH! And the doorman had a hamburger from a fast food place. I smelled the wrapper. Extra onions. No cheese, though." Butterbean looked at them hopefully. "Does that help?"

Walt shot Oscar a warning look. "Yes, thank you. Anything about Mrs. Food?"

Butterbean frowned. "Well, no."

"Did the girl say anything?"

Butterbean perked up. "Yes. But it was mostly 'hurry up' and 'do your business.' I don't think she was talking about Mrs. Food. It was all very cryptic."

"Yes. A mystery," Oscar sighed.

Walt turned to Oscar. "So now what?"

"Emergency meeting," Oscar said. "Now I'm not going to pretend our situation isn't bad. But we shouldn't overreact. We just need to determine how bad."

"It's more than bad," Walt said, slowly licking a paw. "It's really bad."

Oscar rolled his eyes. "Well, maybe not. I saw a news story just the other day about a dog who lost his person, and he inherited millions of dollars. Millions! He even inherited a new person to take care of him!"

"Lucky dog. What's your point?" Walt didn't even pause in her licking.

"Mrs. Food is very responsible—I'm sure she's made provisions for us."

Walt shook her head. "Nope. Sorry."

Oscar looked hurt. "Walt, surely it's worth a look. There are probably papers."

Walt stopped licking. "No, it's not. Because yes, there are papers, and no, we're not in them."

"What? How do you know?" Butterbean gasped. This conversation was moving too fast for her. Walt should have given a spoiler alert at least.

"I live in the office, people. You think I don't go through her papers? It gets boring around here. I've been through everything in there at least three times. I know her passwords. I know her secrets."

"Mrs. Food has secrets?" Butterbean gasped again. She couldn't believe she'd been so blind. First the rats, now secrets? The whole day had just been one cruel blow after another.

"Well, no, that's my point. Mrs. Food has no secrets from me. She also has no provisions for us. She's only made provisions for the Feral Cats Charitable Foundation and *Dog Fancy Magazine*. And unless I'm mistaken, that's not us."

"But . . . but . . ." Oscar sputtered. He thought he'd considered everything. He had a carefully planned set of talking points. His whole speech was ruined. Oscar's feathers drooped. "Well, then I don't know what to say. We're not overreacting. We're doomed."

"We're not doomed," Walt said. "We have options. We just need to make a plan."

"But how?" Butterbean said. "What is there to do?" If Oscar said they were doomed, they were pretty much doomed.

Walt twitched her tail. "Like I said, I know Mrs. Food's secrets. I can use her computer. I'm not a fast typist, but I can do it. I can order things online. At least I think I can."

"What things? Toys?" Butterbean wagged her tail so hard that her butt almost lifted off the floor. She loved new toys.

"I was thinking food. We can have things delivered. That will tide us over until her credit card runs out, at least. All we have to do is figure out a way to open the door and get the boxes."

Oscar shook his head. "That only works if we can get Bob off our backs. Whatever we do, we have to do it fast. In a week."

"Give or take," Butterbean said solemnly. "More or less."

"I'll deal with Bob," Walt said, her eyes gleaming. "I could go for the eyes. Still an option."

"Yes. Well." Oscar cleared his throat. "Even with Bob out of the way, as I see it, our options are limited. Option one? Get jobs. Or option two, become independently wealthy. Personally, I prefer option two."

"I could get a job!" Butterbean said. "I've seen the commercials, work from home! I'm at home, I could work. Maybe I could do that?"

Oscar shifted on his perch. "That's a nice thought, Butterbean, but what kind of work do you think you could do?"

Butterbean hesitated, thinking back over the job descriptions she'd seen listed. Now that she thought about it, she wasn't sure she was really qualified for any of them. She had zero teaching experience. And she didn't even know what coding and transcription were. "Or maybe you could work? A phone job? Since you speak Human?"

"I can also speak Human," Walt grumbled. "In a sense. There's software for speaking Human. I could use that."

"EXCUSE ME," a tiny voice said from across the room. "Would you mind either SPEAKING UP or opening our cage? It's kind of hard to hear you."

Butterbean gasped. "We can't let them out!"

"What do you think they're going to do?" Oscar asked.

"RAT THINGS." Butterbean shuddered. Like it wasn't obvious.

"We'll have to risk it. They're in the same boat we are." Walt hesitated. "And Butterbean, you know that's a figure of speech. There's no boat."

"Of course there's not," Butterbean scoffed. She knew they weren't in a boat. She wouldn't have even suspected it if Walt hadn't said that they were.

"Never mind, we'll handle it," Polo called. "Marco, give me a boost."

Marco held out his hands like a step, and Polo launched herself up like a tiny acrobat onto the top of the water bottle.

"HRRRRRRUUUUUUUNNNNNNGGG," Polo grunted, lying on her back and shoving the top of the cage with her feet. Slowly the lid shifted to the side.

Butterbean's jaw dropped. Those rats could be in the circus.

"Good job, Polo," Marco said, scrambling up to the top of the bottle and giving her a high five.

"Thanks," Polo said, climbing up onto the lid and dusting herself off.

"You mean you can just GET OUT?" Butterbean said.

"You don't think we stay in there all the time, do you?" Marco said.

"That would be ridiculous," Polo agreed.

"WHAT?" Butterbean yelped.

"Can we get back to business?" Oscar said, frowning at Butterbean. He'd learned to unlock his cage when he was just a fledgling with pin feathers. He didn't see why rats would be any different. (Except for the pin feathers.) "Now, the job option is certainly something we can explore. But since the independently wealthy option is preferable, I think our first move should be to take stock of our assets and see where we stand."

"What?" Butterbean cocked her head. "What does that mean?"

"One of us may own something of value. We won't know until we see what we have. Now, everyone gather your treasures, and we'll reconvene here in ten minutes. Again, we might be worrying needlessly."

"You just don't want to get a job," Walt smirked.

"You couldn't have told us this BEFORE we climbed out of our cage?" Marco rolled his eyes.

"Our treasures aren't exactly lying around the apartment, you know." Polo shook her head.

"Apologies," Oscar said, nodding to the rats. "Ten minutes."

The animals scattered, grumbling quietly to themselves. Oscar was bossy, but he had a point. In ten minutes they would know whether they would be living the life of luxury or making telemarketing calls. Or worse.

– 5 –

"So," Oscar said, looking around the circle. "I have to admit this doesn't look promising."

The animals had collected their personal treasures from their hidden stashes and were hovering over them protectively. They all looked very proud, but Oscar had been watching as they made their piles, and he felt a heavy weight in the pit of his stomach. He had expected the piles to be, well, bigger.

"I'll start," Oscar said. "It's not much. There aren't many places to hide things in my cage. So. I have a half dollar—very shiny, if I do say so myself. I have a small silver key. And the pièce de résistance—an earring." He pushed the silver filigree earring forward with one claw.

Butterbean choked back an indignant bark. "Hey, that belongs to Mrs. Food!" Butterbean sniffed the earring. It smelled just like her. Well, Mrs. Food with a whiff of birdcage.

"Yes. Well. You remember that day she lost it? After she'd gone out, I spotted it in between the sofa cushions. I planned to return it if she looked for it again, but she never did. So I decided it was mine."

"Oooh, silvery," Polo said.

"Ooohhh," Marco echoed.

"It is very shiny," Butterbean agreed. "It must be valuable."

"One earring?" Walt said, shaking her head. "I'm not so sure about that."

"It's a start," Oscar said stiffly. "Now what do you have, Walt? You must have something much better than a paltry earring."

"You could say that," Walt smirked. "I have an unexpired credit card, and THIS!" She whipped a pair of socks out from behind her back.

"OOOH." Butterbean's nose quivered. "Are those . . . socks?"

"Not just any socks, Butterbean," Walt said dramatically. "COMPRESSION socks."

"OOOH." Butterbean edged closer to sniff. "What does that mean?"

"I'm not sure exactly," Walt admitted. "But I heard Mrs. Food say that they are WORTH THEIR WEIGHT IN GOLD."

"Hmm." Oscar examined the socks. They looked like regular socks to him. "And you think she meant that literally?"

"Don't you?" Walt looked shocked. "Add it to the list!"

Oscar hesitated, then made a note. "Assets so far: one earring, a credit card, and um, special socks. Now. Marco? Polo?"

Marco and Polo exchanged glances, and then Polo gave Marco a tiny shove forward. He was holding a small piece of corn in his hands. "I have this corn. But see? It's shaped like a rat head. Isn't that interesting?"

"It looks like Marco!" Polo piped up. "Show them, Marco!"

Marco gave the rat equivalent of a blush and then held the piece of corn up next to his face.

"You have to squinch up your eyes to see it," he said shyly.

Walt, Oscar, and Butterbean squinched up their eyes.

"Oh yeah . . ." Butterbean said. "I see it. That's the nose there. It looks just like you!"

"Right," Marco said, embarrassed. "I was just

thinking, it's not every day you see a piece of corn shaped like a rat head."

Walt and Oscar exchanged a look.

"That's true," Oscar said.

"Striking," Walt said. "But I don't know how much of a market there is for rat-head corn."

"Put it on the list," Polo said, waving her paws at Oscar. "It's an asset."

Oscar sighed. "Yes. One rat-head corn. Done."

"I don't have anything that good," Polo sighed. "I just have two things. A thimble and a piece of string." She pushed the thimble and a long piece of red string into the middle of the circle. "I don't know what you can do with them. I was thinking maybe a thimble hat, but it kept falling off."

"Right," Oscar said. He was looking more and more depressed with each new item. "String. Thimble. Check." He sighed heavily. "Butterbean?"

"Oooh, I've got so much good stuff," Butterbean started. She opened her mouth to go on, but the sound of a key in the lock made her snap it shut again.

"Quick! Back to your regular places. Act normal!" Oscar screeched, leaping for his cage. He'd just reached it when the door opened, and everyone froze midscramble.

"Hey, guys, just forgot my . . ." The girl trailed off

as she stared into the room. She'd expected the animals to be startled or excited when she came in, but she hadn't expected ... this.

The two rats were lounging casually against the wall of their aquarium, except for some reason it looked like they were on the *outside* of the cage instead of the inside. The bird was perched in his cage as usual, except it looked like he was holding the door shut with one foot. And the dog and cat were sitting bolt upright and staring at her. Blinking innocently. Like they were hiding something.

They were the weirdest pets she'd ever seen.

"My, um, bag. I left my bag from before. So. See you guys tomorrow."

None of the animals moved. They all just stared. The girl swung her bag over her shoulder, accidentally catching one of the sparkly buttons on her sweater and ripping it off. Five sets of eyes watched it fall.

Polo had to be physically restrained by Marco, who covered by grinning like a maniac.

The girl hesitated at the door. "I was just by myself, so . . . I thought you might want some company? I could hang out here, if you want. Or not."

She waited. Surely at least one of the pets would do something close to normal pet behavior. But nope, just staring and blinking and lounging.

Her shoulders sagged. "Okay, then. It was just a thought. Um. Bye." She gave a little wave as she slipped through the door, locking it behind her.

"MINE!" Polo shrieked as the door closed, wrenching herself loose from Marco's grasp and throwing herself at the sparkly button. "Isn't this the most beautiful thing EVER? It's like she wanted me to have it!" She held it up so it caught the light. "She made eye contact with me. She wanted to be my friend. It's practically a GIFT! For ME!"

"Better let her have it. She'll fight you for it," Marco said under his breath.

"We were such good actors!" Butterbean said, tail thumping. "I don't think she suspected anything was up. We all looked so casual! Hey, Oscar, maybe we could be in MOVIES!"

"Right," Walt said, shifting uncomfortably and watching the door. That leaving-the-bag trick wasn't an accident. She wouldn't be surprised if the girl made another appearance. That girl was definitely suspicious. Something was up with her anyway. Walt didn't think they had a lot of time. "So show us what you've got, Butterbean. Anything good?"

"Well, yeah, lots." She pushed her pile forward. "Check it out. I'm rich."

Oscar hopped forward and sorted the pile with his foot. "Hmm. A broken calculator, a comb, a nickel . . ."

"Canadian," Walt sniffed.

"Five cents, Canadian. A chewed-up toothbrush and a . . . Butterbean, is this a piece of toast?"

"It sure is! From two weeks ago! I'm saving it."

"Hmm. Toast. A bar of hotel soap . . ."

"From when she went away for TWO DAYS. I saved that, too. It smells lemony."

Oscar didn't even dignify that with a response. Riches weren't "lemony." He pushed the soap aside and continued. "A bottle cap and . . . underpants?"

"I have my own UNDERWEAR!" Butterbean forced herself to stay seated. They were in a serious situation. She had to keep her cool.

"And that's valuable how?" Oscar said. He wasn't trying to be a jerk. But it was a pair of underpants.

"Oh come ON!" Butterbean rolled her eyes at him. "People are CRAZY for underpants. They NEVER let you play with them. And they ALWAYS have them. These must be super valuable."

"She has a point," Walt agreed. "Mrs. Food never lets me NEAR her underpants."

Oscar looked skeptical. "Noted. Is that all?"

"Isn't that ENOUGH? I've got some great stuff here." Butterbean looked offended.

"It's great stuff, Bean. Except maybe not the underpants and the . . . um . . . toast." Oscar looked queasy. "But . . ."

"But it's not stuff that helps us out a lot right now," Walt said. "Not like my credit card. And compression socks," she finished, under her breath.

"So," Oscar sighed. "It looks as though our hopes of becoming independently wealthy are over. Which is unfortunate, because I don't think there are a lot of job opportunities for birds right now. But nevertheless, I will—" He stopped suddenly, cocking his head. He hopped forward and tilted it to the other side.

"Oscar?" Walt said. She hoped he wasn't losing it. The stress was enough to make any bird crack.

"Butterbean?" Oscar said, taking another hop closer. "Butterbean, what is that?"

Butterbean looked around with a panicked expression on her face. "What is what? My soap?"

"Not your soap. Under your tail." Oscar's eyes glittered.

Butterbean leaned down and inspected her tail. "OH!" She laughed and scooted her butt an inch to the side. "That's just my coin. I wondered what had happened to it!"

"You were sitting on it." Oscar hopped over to the coin and eyed it with interest.

"Not on purpose. It's small." Butterbean looked offended.

"OOOOOhhhh," Marco said.

"Shiny," Polo said.

"It looks like gold, Butterbean," Oscar said, picking it up and putting it down in front of Walt. "Walt, do you know what this is?"

Walt leaned forward. The coin was small, with a tiny antelope or gazelle on the front. "I know enough to know it's worth a lot," Walt said. "I'll have to do some research to make sure. But it's definitely valuable."

"That's what I thought." Oscar fluffed up his feathers. "Butterbean, where did you get this? You need to tell us everything. Now."

"I was in the lobby," Butterbean started. "It was a while ago. Maybe a few weeks? Or days? I'm not sure. I was waiting to go up in the elevator, and Mrs. Food was talking to Mrs. Third Floor. Then the elevator opened, and Biscuit came out with her owner."

"Haircut Biscuit?" Polo asked.

Butterbean shook her head. "Different Biscuit."

Oscar narrowed his eyes. "Did Biscuit's owner drop the coin?"

"No, it was the other person in the elevator. Some guy. No dog."

"What do you remember about him?" Oscar wished he had a lamp that he could shine on Butterbean while he asked questions. He'd seen that technique on the Television, and it always seemed to work.

Butterbean shrugged. "Nothing. He dropped the coin. And I picked it up and brought it home and hid it with the rest of my stuff."

"Any smells?" Walt said.

"Cologne. Lots of it. It made me sneeze." Butterbean wrinkled her nose at the thought.

"Have you smelled it before?"

"Yes, in the elevator."

"So he's a resident of the building," Oscar said slowly, tapping his wing against his beak thoughtfully.

"So? What do we care who the guy is?" Walt twitched her tail. If her memory was accurate, that coin was a South African Krugerrand, worth hundreds of dollars. Walt didn't know anyone with hundreds of dollars.

"We care because now I know what we're going to do," Oscar said impatiently. "Reconnaissance begins tomorrow. Butterbean, get your sleep. You've got a big day ahead of you."

"Okay . . ." Butterbean didn't know what reconnaissance was, but she didn't like the sound of it. It sounded hard.

"Reconnaissance? For what? We got the coin! We're set!" Walt said.

"We are not, as you say, set," Oscar said. "But if all goes as planned, we will be. We'll never have to worry about money or our future again."

Walt glared at him.

Oscar sighed. "Walt, if we sell this coin, the money will last us only a short time. But a coin like this, it's not the sort of thing you just drop in a lobby. Not unless you have a lot of them. If I'm correct, the man who lost this coin has a lot of them."

"So?"

"So we'll take them. We're going to pull off a heist."

– 6 –

WHEN THE GIRL ARRIVED THE NEXT MORNING, they were ready. Oscar had worked out their assignments late into the night, and they'd gone over their roles just as the sun was coming up.

"Butterbean, walk duty."

"Check." Butterbean's tongue flopped out of the side of her mouth. Oscar ignored it.

"Polo, you're with Butterbean. You know what you have to do. Marco, general surveillance."

"Check!" Polo and Marco said at the same time. Then they giggled.

"Jinx!" they said at the same time.

"Jinx!"

"Jinx!"

Oscar frowned. This was no time for giggling. He cleared his throat. The jinxing stopped. "Walt, entrance and exit facilitation. Logistics."

"Check." Walt licked a paw.

"I'll be monitoring the feeds and assisting as needed." Oscar paused. "Check." (He just wanted to say "check" too.)

Oscar patted the remote with one wing. The Strathmore apartment building had security cameras that residents could watch on the Television. Oscar had never been a fan—watching people come in and out of the building was not his idea of fun—but it was exactly what they needed to pull off a successful heist. If there was a stash of treasure hidden in the Strathmore, they would find it. And it would all be his.

Oscar cringed at himself. Theirs. Not his. Theirs.

"She's coming," Walt said from her post by the front door. "Polo? You know what to do."

"This seems weird." Polo laughed nervously, scurrying over to Butterbean. "Hope you're not ticklish."

Polo slicked her forehead and side fur down, then leaned up and grabbed a long piece of the hair on Butterbean's underside. Luckily, since Butterbean was a short dog, it wasn't that hard to do.

Polo hesitated. "Wait . . ."

"Do you need a boost?" Marco whispered.

"A boost? She's not tall," Polo scoffed.

"I know I'm short, okay?" Butterbean muttered. "Rub it in, why don't you."

"Then what is it?"

"It's not that. It's . . . my button! I can't leave my button!" Polo looked panicked.

"It'll be fine. Nobody will take it," Marco whispered, looking at the door. He could hear noises coming from the hallway.

"No, I need it!" Polo was sounding frantic. Marco had seen her that way before. The last time, she'd spent half the day digging in the corner of the aquarium, and all of their cedar chips had ended up in a dune on top of their food dish.

"But you can't hold a button and hold on to Butterbean at the same time!" Walt said impatiently.

"Here," Marco said. "How's this?" He grabbed Polo's red string and looped it through the hole in the button. Then he tied it quickly around Polo's neck. "Okay now?"

"Thanks," Polo sighed. "I just . . . I didn't want to leave it."

"I get it," Marco said. "I feel the same way about my rat-head corn."

"Great, problem solved, now get up there!" Walt said, eyes on the door.

Polo patted the sparkling button around her neck and then grabbed Butterbean's fur again. In one quick motion, she pulled herself up so she was hanging under Butterbean's tummy.

"I've . . . I've got a rat on me," Butterbean whispered.

"It's the plan, remember? You agreed to this. It's what we have to do," Walt said.

"Yes, but . . . I have a rat," Butterbean said. "On me."

"Don't make any sudden moves. Your hair is kind of slippery," Polo said from her position under Butterbean's stomach.

"I condition," Butterbean said.

"I can tell," Polo said. "I just hope we can pull this off." She hoisted herself up higher and grabbed on tighter with her feet.

A key turned in the lock.

"Showtime," Walt said under her breath.

Walt had given them all a little acting advice, so they looked much more natural than they had the night before.

Butterbean was standing in the middle of the living room, positioning herself in a way that didn't show off the rat on her tummy.

Marco was sprawled on top of a pile of cedar chips in the aquarium, doing his best to look like two rats.

Oscar was sitting on his perch reading the clean parts of yesterday's paper.

Walt was sitting on the coffee table, licking her foot and watching the door. All in all, they were doing an admirable job of looking casual. (Except for Butterbean, that is. But they were hoping she just looked like she really needed to pee, and not like she had a rat suspended from her stomach.)

"Hey, guys." The girl peered into the room. "Doing okay this morning?"

In her best impression of a regular house cat, Walt ignored her completely.

Oscar hopped on his perch and raked his beak against the bars of his cage. Butterbean wagged her tail enthusiastically.

"Hey!" Polo said in a muffled voice. "Watch it with the tail!"

"Sorry," Butterbean whispered. She stopped wagging and let her tongue loll out of her mouth instead.

"How 'bout I take you out first and then check on the others, okay?" The girl clipped Butterbean's leash onto her collar.

"Just as we planned," Walt said softly. "You know what you have to do, Butterbean! Good luck, Polo!"

Butterbean waddled slowly to the door, trying her best to ignore the weird weight on her stomach. "Wow, you okay?" the girl asked. "Really need to go, huh?"

Butterbean attempted a smile, but just managed to look constipated.

The girl bent down to pet her and then frowned. "Hey, wait. What is—"

"Walt! Distraction!" Oscar said quickly.

Walt stopped licking her foot and started hacking up a hairball.

The girl stood up quickly as Walt convulsed on the edge of the coffee table.

"Um. You okay, cat? Walt?"

Walt's hairball splatted onto the carpet.

"Okay, so all better now." The girl looked grossed out. "I'll take care of that when we get back. Come on, dog." She tugged the leash and hurried Butterbean out into the hallway.

As the door swung shut behind them, Walt leaped to her feet. Sprinting across the room, she scooped up Butterbean's rawhide chew and pushed it into the gap, preventing the door from closing completely. The girl didn't notice.

"Bingo," Walt said. "Tape, Oscar?"

Oscar flew into the kitchen and tore a piece of

tape off the dispenser. Then he flew over to Walt, who carefully took it from his beak and taped it over the latch on the side of the door. They repeated the process until they were sure the latch was completely covered. "Better safe than sorry," Oscar said.

After patting the tape in place to make sure it was secure, Walt batted the rawhide chew out of the way and let the door swing shut. Then she jumped up onto the handle and opened it again.

"Nice work," Oscar said, flapping his wings happily. "And totally disgusting distraction, by the way."

Walt grinned.

Part one of the plan was a success.

Outside at the elevator, Butterbean wasn't feeling quite so optimistic. There was a weird new stain by the stairway door that she was just itching to investigate, but she didn't think it was appropriate with a rat hanging from her tummy. Even a nice rat.

In fact, now that she thought about it, there were a couple of other things she wasn't sure she could do with a rat hanging from her tummy. Two things, in fact. Two very important things.

"Polo," Butterbean hissed. "What do we do about . . . you know."

"What?" Polo said, trying to maintain her grip on Butterbean's hair.

"YOU know," Butterbean said again.

"I don't," Polo said.

"If you're under there . . ." Butterbean said. "And I need to . . . you know."

Polo didn't say anything.

"I'm on a WALK, Polo."

"OH!" Polo stopped adjusting her grip and just dangled. "We need to rethink this."

"I don't want to pee on you!" Butterbean said in a low wail.

"I appreciate that," Polo said. "We need to figure this out fast."

The original plan had been for Butterbean and Polo to go out for Butterbean's usual walk, and when Butterbean smelled the mystery coin owner, Polo would drop down on the ground and investigate. But they hadn't really considered the actual purpose of Butterbean's morning walk. Until now.

For the first time in her life, Butterbean was glad the elevator in their building was so slow.

Polo tried to think. "Okay, so let's be honest. It's unlikely that you'll smell the man outside of the building, right? I mean, you definitely found the coin in the lobby?"

"Right," Butterbean said, craning her head down to look between her legs at Polo.

"Keep your head up! I'm not here, remember?" Polo squeaked.

"Right, not there. Yes, he was definitely in this building." Butterbean was almost 90 percent sure of that. Maybe a little less. Maybe 80 percent.

"Good. Is there a hiding place in the lobby? Trash can, potted plant, anything like that?"

"Yes, both," Butterbean said softly.

"Okay, good. This is what we'll do. I'll wait there while you head out to do your ... um ... stuff. Then I'll grab you when you come back in. I'll keep an eye on things in the lobby while you're gone. Heck, maybe I'll spot him myself." Not that it was likely, but if it meant not getting peed on, Polo was all for it.

"Okay, got it. New plan," Butterbean said nervously.

"Look, here's the elevator," the girl said, patting Butterbean on the head. "It's okay, little guy!"

Butterbean barely noticed the head pat. She just hoped the girl was right.

Oscar pecked at the remote in the living room, periodically craning his neck to peer at the Television. "I know one of these is the surveillance channel. We'll be able to monitor them as soon as I find it."

"I should've just gone with her. I don't like this. Too much could go wrong," Walt said, pacing back and forth.

"You could hardly have hidden on Butterbean's stomach," Oscar said, rolling his eyes. Walt was a little bit of a control freak. "Now move. I think you're blocking the signal." Walt stalked over to the sofa and sat down.

"Don't worry, they'll be okay. Polo will keep

Butterbean on track," Marco said, munching on a sunflower seed in front of the TV.

"Found it!" Oscar said, sitting back and eyeing the screen. The channel was divided into four different views from four different cameras. One showed the lobby and the elevators, one showed the front entrance to the building, one showed the back entrance, and one showed the garage entrance. "We can ignore that last one. I don't think they're going to drive anywhere."

"You never know," Walt said darkly. "It's Butterbean. Anything could happen."

"Look! There they are!" Marco squealed. "They're on TV!" He hopped up and rushed to the screen, scattering sunflower shells in his wake.

"So far so good," Oscar said. "The plan is going off without a hitch."

"Don't jinx it," Walt said, flicking a piece of sunflower shell off of her tail.

On the screen, a black-and-white version of the girl and Butterbean walked out of the elevator and crossed the lobby.

"Wait—what was that?" Oscar said. What looked like a small black smudge had dropped onto the floor behind Butterbean. Oscar squinted at the screen. "Something's wrong. Oh no. Tell me Butterbean didn't just—"

"It's POLO!" Marco shrieked. "See that sparkle? Hi, Polo!" He waved wildly at the screen.

"Going off without a hitch, huh?" Walt shook her head at Oscar. "I'm pretty sure the rat wasn't supposed to fall off in the lobby."

"No, that was on purpose. Look!" Marco said. "See her duck and weave? That's her evasive maneuver. She did that on purpose."

The little black smudge on the screen was, in fact, ducking and weaving across the lobby before finally taking cover beside a potted plant. No one in the lobby seemed to notice.

"Can we tape this? Polo's on TV!" Marco jumped up and down.

"I don't think . . ." Oscar looked uncertain.

"Ooohh! Did she wave? I think she waved!" Marco squealed and waved back. "Hi, Polo!"

"She can't hear you," Walt said.

"She did not wave." Oscar suppressed a groan. He should've known better than to work with rats. "She seems to have hidden. Why, I have no idea." He snapped his beak shut. His perfect plan, ruined by a rat with weak arms.

"Maybe Butterbean conditions too much?" Marco said.

"Maybe Polo needs to work out," Oscar said.

"Cool it. It's not over," Walt said, twitching her tail. "They could still gather the information we need. Just keep an eye on them both."

"Easier said than done," Oscar said grimly, watching the blurry security screen. When this was all over, whoever was in charge of those cameras would be getting a very strongly worded complaint letter.

Polo was definitely hard to see. Only the occasional sparkle from the button around her neck gave her position away. And Butterbean, seemingly oblivious to her lost cargo, was slowly ambling out of camera range.

Oscar gritted his beak and hoped for the best.

"I made it. I MADE IT!" Polo shrieked from her position next to the potted plant. "Go get 'em, Butterbean!"

"See you after I poop!" Butterbean called over her shoulder.

"Okay, bye!" Polo shrieked again. Then she dashed out of the shadow for a second, waving her tiny hand wildly at the ceiling, where she imagined the security camera probably was. (She was a little off.) "Hi, Marco!"

Butterbean couldn't help but feel relieved that she didn't need to worry about a rat on her tummy anymore. Bathroom difficulties aside, it made it harder to concentrate on smelling things. And there were so many smells to focus on. Trash smells, cleaning smells, food smells, perfume smells, and that was just inside the lobby. To be honest, there were so many smells, Butterbean wasn't sure she'd recognize the mystery coin owner even if he was standing right next to her.

She had to focus. She had to get this right. If she didn't, Oscar would never let her forget it. Plus, she'd have to come out with a rat on her tummy again, and she definitely didn't want that.

Luckily, Polo had lots of good ideas, so they'd come up with another new plan, just in case she didn't find the guy outside. Plan B. But neither of them wanted to try Plan B. (It wasn't even Oscar approved.)

"You walking this little stinker now, Madison?" the doorman said, smiling as he got up to open the door.

Butterbean stopped walking in astonishment. Stinker?

"For now. Until her person comes back," the girl, apparently named Madison, said smiling. Butterbean stifled an outraged yip and suppressed her canine instincts, which were to go for the doorman's bony ankles. Probably the wolf in her. But still, STINKER? And the Madison girl didn't even defend her. The Coin Man better be worth it.

"Haven't seen that aunt of yours recently. She okay?"

"Um, sure. Just busy I guess." Madison shifted. She seemed less happy about that line of conversation than she had about the stinker comment. Weird.

"Well, tell her I said not to be such a stranger, okay?" the doorman said, leaning on the doorframe, blocking Butterbean and Madison's way out. "Tell her to stop by and see her old pal."

"Um. Yeah. I'll tell her," Madison mumbled, looking at the floor.

"Good, good," Mr. Doorman said, continuing his lounging act. He didn't look like he was ever planning to move.

Butterbean frowned. Something was up with Madison, but Butterbean didn't think it was the stinker insult. Butterbean wuffled under her breath. Sounded like secrets.

That was it. She'd had enough. She had work to do, and she really did need to pee.

In one big dramatic flourish, Butterbean started to hunker down, like she was going to let loose and pee in the lobby. (As if. Biscuit would never let her live that down.)

Mr. Doorman immediately stopped his lounging and sprang into action.

"Oh geez, better get that dog outside, quick," he said, jumping back and shooing Butterbean toward the exit with his hat. She had to do a little hop to avoid getting whacked in the butt, but it was worth it to get moving again. Butterbean shot him a snippy over-the-shoulder look, snout in the air, and bounced outside.

Mr. Doorman wasn't important. Madison's secrets weren't important. Butterbean couldn't let herself get distracted. What was important was the smell. The Coin Man smell. This was it. It was up to her now. Sniffer powers, activate.

Polo watched Butterbean and Madison leave the building, and then she hung out under the potted plant, trying to look casual. Which wasn't as easy as it sounded—she didn't know what to do with her hands. But it didn't really matter anyway, because no one was looking at her.

Polo was starting to have doubts about the whole plan, actually. She'd originally thought the hanging-under-the-dog's-tummy part was going to be the worst part, but now that she'd had a little alone time with the plant, she was noticing some problems. The whole thing depended on Butterbean and Polo bumping into the Coin Man. But what if they didn't?

Polo couldn't help but notice that nobody in the

lobby looked like their coin guy. In fact, there weren't that many people at all, except for the doorman guy sitting on his stool humming along with the Muzak. And Polo. And she wasn't smelling anything that smelled like gold coins.

At least she and Butterbean had come up with a new plan of their own. Plan B. But she sure didn't want to do that. Heck, Polo wasn't even sure they COULD do it.

Polo leaned against a leafy branch (which didn't even look real, now that she had time to examine it) and laughed at herself softly. She was being so silly. Oscar was great at planning. Much better than Polo. That bathroom thing had been just a weird accident. His plan would work fine. Butterbean had probably smelled the guy by now. There was nothing to worry about.

※ ※ ※ ※ ※ ※ ※ ※ ※ ※

Butterbean had not smelled the guy. She hadn't smelled anything remotely like the guy, and she'd even taken extra time to smell the newspaper box and the bus stop bench. Nothing. (Well, not nothing. Lots of somethings. Biscuit, for one. But no Coin Man.)

She'd dawdled as much as she could doing her business, but unless the girl Madison wanted to do another lap around the block, the next stop would be back inside. And Plan B.

Butterbean decided to try for another lap around the block.

"Oh no, that's it for you," Madison said, jerking on the leash as Butterbean tried to hustle past the building entrance. "I've got to get myself to school, okay? I can't walk you all day. I can't even be late, or they might try to call my aunt and then . . . well, I just can't be late." Madison leaned down and pushed Butterbean in the direction of the building.

Butterbean hardly thought pushing was necessary. She gave up and slunk toward the entrance. Maybe the man would be in the lobby. He probably was. He was probably talking to Mr. Doorman right that minute, dropping gold coins left and right.

Madison held the door open and ushered Butterbean inside.

Butterbean stopped in the doorway and did a quick scan of the lobby. High-heel feet with too much perfume. Biscuit's dog walker, the one with the squeaky shoes. Polo, under the plant, waving like a maniac. That was it. No Coin Man, no coin smells. Nothing. She slumped against the doorframe.

Butterbean was a failure.

"Get moving, okay? Wow, you're a weird dog,"

Madison said, scooching Butterbean over to the elevator.

Butterbean was a failure and a weird dog.

She had a hard time looking Polo in the eye. But when she finally did, Polo didn't look disappointed. She looked freaked out. And to be honest, a little crazy.

"That's it, then?" Polo asked. If they were going with Plan B, they had to do it now.

"That's it." Butterbean hung her head.

Polo took a deep breath. "Okay. Initiate Plan B."

-7-

"So, what do you think?" Walt asked Oscar as they watched the surveillance feed.

"I think it looks great! So exciting! This is better than a movie!" Marco said enthusiastically. "I just wish we had a piece of popcorn to go with it!"

Oscar shifted from one foot to the other as he side-eyed Marco. "It doesn't appear that the man with the coins has been found."

"No," Walt agreed.

They'd watched as Butterbean distracted the doorman and went outside. They'd waited, trying to catch a glimpse of Polo hidden under the potted plant. But now Butterbean was back, and the only thing she seemed to be doing was standing and sniffing the lobby.

"I don't think anyone there looks like our guy," Walt said.

"I think that one's a lady," Marco said, pointing at the screen.

"What I can't understand is why Polo and Butterbean didn't stick to the plan," Oscar said. "Why was Polo under that plant? Why didn't she go outside with Butterbean?" Oscar ruffled his feathers and sighed loudly. "Well, that's it, then."

"Try again tomorrow?" Walt asked.

"What else is there to do?" Oscar shrugged his wings.

They didn't know about Plan B.

They watched as Butterbean and the girl waited for the elevator. When the doors opened, Oscar leaned forward to peck the remote to turn the Television off. But a paw across the face stopped him cold.

"Walt, what—"

"What are they DOING?" Walt gasped. She jumped to her feet and rushed forward to press her nose against the screen.

Oscar's jaw dropped. "Are they INSANE?"

Plan B had started.

Butterbean felt like maybe this wasn't such a good idea. It had seemed okay when Polo had suggested it in the elevator, but that was before they thought they'd actually have to do it. When Butterbean's biggest concern was keeping a rat from hitching a ride on her tummy while she peed. That didn't seem like such a big deal now that Plan B was about to go into effect.

"You ready?" Polo squeaked from her position under the plant. She wasn't getting back onto Butterbean's tummy. That part of the plan was OVER.

"Ready," Butterbean yipped, stealing a peek up at Madison. The girl was twirling the end of the leash and shooting nervous glances at Mr. Doorman. She wasn't paying attention to Butterbean.

Good.

The elevator bell dinged in the lobby.

The doors opened. The elevator was empty.

"NOW!" Polo shrieked, rushing quickly through the open elevator doors.

"GOT IT!" Butterbean shrieked back, jerking the leash out of Madison's hand as she ran at top speed away from the elevator.

"Butterbean, NOOOO!" Madison yelled.

Butterbean skidded across the lobby, slid into the plate glass window, and bounced off, turning back just as Madison started running toward her. Perfect.

Butterbean skidded between Madison's legs and tumbled into the elevator just as the doors started to close.

"Grab my leash! Grab my leash!" Butterbean squealed. Polo desperately tugged at the leash, which was lying partly in the lobby and partly inside the elevator, still attached to Butterbean.

"I'm trying!" Polo said, jerking the leash inside just as the doors slammed shut.

"Whew!" Polo hunched over with her hands on her knees and took a deep breath. "Okay, now hurry, give me a boost!"

Butterbean stood with her paws on the elevator panel and tried not to give in to the heebie-jeebies as Polo raced up her back and perched on her head. Paws flying, Polo pushed the button for every single floor.

"You can skip four—that's us," Butterbean said. She was trying to keep her head still so Polo wouldn't lose her balance, but she wanted to see what Polo was doing.

"Too late," Polo said, settling back between Butterbean's ears. "I pushed them all. Now get ready."

"Ready," Butterbean said. She positioned herself in front of the elevator door, waiting.

Polo slid down onto the floor. "Hold on, let me fix this leash so it won't get caught. If you get strangled, it'll give me nightmares."

"Me too," Butterbean said. She shuddered just thinking about it.

Polo looped the leash around Butterbean's collar so that the end wasn't dragging anymore. She patted it carefully as she watched the elevator numbers. "Now go."

The elevator dinged as it reached the second floor. "Second floor," a disembodied lady's voice said.

"That's really creepy," Polo muttered.

"You should hear her say 'lobby,'" Butterbean said. "Gets me every time."

The doors opened.

"You know what to do!" Polo shrieked, throwing herself in front of the elevator door. Butterbean had said that her rat-sized body should be enough to keep the door from closing, but until they tested it, they couldn't be sure. And now that Polo thought about it, getting squished in the elevator door was something else that would give her nightmares.

Butterbean raced out of the elevator and then ran up and down the hallway, pausing only to sniff under each door.

"Biscuit!" she yelled at the first door. "Teacher Man!" she yelled at the second. "Too Many Kids!" she yelled at the third. "Old Mothball Lady!" she yelled at the fourth. "All clear."

"Great!" Polo said, bracing herself against the elevator door. "Now hurry! This thing is trying to move!"

Butterbean rushed back into the elevator, skidding into the wall just as Polo leaped inside and let the door slide shut.

"We're like superheroes! This is so fun!" Butterbean panted, her tongue hanging out of the side of her mouth.

"Yeah, well, I hope you keep feeling that way, because we've got seven more floors to go. Get ready!"

Butterbean took her position in front of the door and shot out of the elevator as the doors opened, quickly making the circuit. "Mrs. Third Floor! Man With Stinky Sweat Socks! Perfume Lady! Lots of Cats!" She yelled at each apartment before turning and skidding back into the elevator. "We're awesome! We could do this professionally."

Polo suppressed a grin. "We are pretty great, huh? Okay, get ready for the next flooooor!" she yelled, diving into the gap to hold the elevator door. Plan B was looking like a winner. Oscar was going to be so surprised when he found out.

Oscar was already surprised. At that moment he was doing some pretty serious stress plucking of his under feathers and trying not to fly off the handle (literally). "WHAT ARE THEY DOING!" he screamed. "What's HAPPENING!"

The lobby was in an uproar. The last they'd seen of Polo and Butterbean was when Polo did a mad dash into the elevator and Butterbean looked like she'd gone crazy, racing around the lobby and then disappearing into the elevator just as the doors closed.

The girl had been knocked off her feet when Butterbean raced in between her legs, and she'd spent a few minutes gesturing wildly at the doorman before racing to a door at the end of the lobby, opening it, and disappearing.

"The stairway," Walt said softly.

The doorman had looked concerned for a few minutes, until a lady with a big hat came in. Then he seemed to go back to his usual self, smiling and holding the door like nothing had happened.

"Wow, did you see that?" Marco bobbed up and down nervously. "Maybe they've gone CRAZY! Or maybe they're found the coins and they're cutting us out of the loop! Oh man, it's just like a real action movie! We've been double-crossed! They've gone ROGUE!" He hugged his rat-head corn in excitement. "Isn't it awesome?"

"We haven't been double-crossed. It'll be fine," Walt said slowly. "I think."

"Wait, what's that?" They could hear the sound of the elevator dinging in the hallway, followed by the sound of frantic barking.

"That's Butterbean," Oscar said, flying to front door and hovering awkwardly. He'd never been good at using the peephole.

"That Workout Lady Who Gives Me Snacks! The Airplane Man Who's Never Home! The Guy Who Smokes Cigars. Us! Hi, guys, be back in a sec!"

Butterbean barked at the doorway. Then they heard the elevator doors close. There was silence.

"So it sounds like there's a new plan?" Walt said, ears back and eyes wide.

"Those two are going to ruin everything," Oscar groaned as he dropped back to the floor.

Butterbean slumped in the back of the elevator and waited for the doors to open. Polo leaned against the wall next to the door. They weren't having so much fun anymore.

Butterbean had done the circuit over and over, sniffing every apartment on every floor, and so far they hadn't even gotten one whiff of the Coin Man.

"Just two floors left, Bean," Polo said, watching the numbers.

"I know," Butterbean said.

"And you're sure you haven't smelled him?"

"I'm sure." Butterbean hadn't smelled anything like the Coin Man smell. She was starting to think she'd imagined him. Maybe he didn't even live in the building. He could've been visiting. He could've dropped the coin in the lobby, gone away, and never come back.

The door opened, and Butterbean trudged out into the hallway while Polo flopped over to block the door. Around the sixth floor she'd realized she didn't have to actually hold the door closed. Lying in front of the sensor worked just as well.

"Patchouli Family. Biscuit. Empty apartment. No, wait—not empty. Pencils? Pretzels? Anyway, not him." Butterbean headed for the last door and took a sniff. "Nope. Axe Body Spray and fish." She didn't even feel like explaining what she'd sniffed anymore. It all seemed so pointless now. And they didn't have a Plan C.

"Okay, one last chance," Polo said, scooting back into the elevator after Butterbean had returned. "If he's not on the top floor, he's not here."

"I know," Butterbean said quietly.

"So," Polo said after a second. "Haircut Biscuit?"

"Different Biscuit."

They didn't say anything else as the elevator climbed to the top floor.

The doors opened.

Butterbean gave Polo a mournful glance as she plodded into the hallway. The top floor wasn't like the other floors. There were only two apartment doors. Butterbean sniffed the first one. "Nope. Furniture polish and incense."

Butterbean turned and looked at the last apartment. Then, taking a deep breath, she marched down the hall.

"Just smell it," Polo said from the elevator.

Butterbean stuck her nose under the door as far as it would go, and then she took a big sniff.

Her head shot up. She looked back at Polo. "I think . . ."

She took another sniff under the door. "Polo. Polo. I think . . ."

The door to the stairway burst open and Madison lurched into the hallway, red faced and panting. "There you are! What did you do that for, you crazy dog?"

She dropped to her knees and hugged Butterbean tightly. "I was so worried about you!"

Butterbean, caught tight in Madison's hug, raised her eyebrows at Polo, who shrugged. Butterbean licked the girl across the forehead.

"We have to get you home, okay?" Madison reached down and examined Butterbean's collar and leash. "How did you get it all twisted like that?"

She had just gotten the leash untangled when the apartment door jerked open.

A tall man with icy blue eyes stared down at them.

Madison's grip on Butterbean tightened. "Oh, um. Hi. I'm sorry. I just . . . see, the dog . . . she got in the elevator . . ." Madison stammered, gesturing back toward the elevator. Polo pressed herself against the elevator door, hoping the man wouldn't notice her.

She shouldn't have worried. He never took his eyes off Madison. And he didn't say a word.

Polo shivered. There was something about his eyes. She was glad he wasn't looking at her.

Madison scrambled to her feet. "So anyway. Sorry to disturb you." She twisted the leash around her hand as she took a step back.

"You should go," the man said, his face stony. "Now."

"Yes, sir," Madison said, backing away toward the elevator. "Leaving. Right now."

She bolted through the open elevator door and jabbed the fourth-floor button, holding her breath until the door had shut.

"I didn't like that guy," Polo said quietly as she crawled into position under Butterbean's tummy.

"He never stopped looking at her, not once. Polo, that was him. The Coin Man," Butterbean whined under her breath. "It was bad, Polo."

"I saw." Polo shuddered. She was glad that she had Butterbean's hair to hide her.

Butterbean kept her eyes on the door. She hardly even noticed the rat hanging from her underside.

"We'll tell Oscar. He'll know what to do." Polo tightened her grip on Butterbean's hair. "We did our part. Oscar will know what to do."

- 8 -

THERE WAS ANOTHER BIG FLAW IN THEIR plan, one that they didn't figure out until they were back in the apartment. They had to keep acting like normal pets until Madison left.

This was harder than it seemed. Oscar didn't think he'd ever seen anyone take so long to clean a litter box.

"Did you have to poop so much, Walt?" Butterbean grumbled, watching Madison hard at work with the litter sifter.

"Can it, Bean," Walt said, not looking at her. "I know you used it too."

"It was an emergency!" Butterbean started to wail, lowering her voice just in time.

Marco and Polo tried desperately to cover up the soiled corner of their cage with clean cedar chips so Madison wouldn't feel the need to change their bedding too. It didn't work.

"Doesn't she need to be somewhere? Talk on the phone to someone? Eat dinner? Do ANYTHING?" Marco said, hiding behind the water bottle and clutching his rat-head corn. "Why is she hanging out with us?"

Polo peered at the girl from behind the food dish. "Something's not right here. It's like she doesn't want to leave." Polo frowned and crouched lower behind the dish. The last thing she wanted was to end up in a tub of sudsy water.

By the time everyone's food and water had been refreshed, the animals were practically twitching with anxiety.

"Okay, well, I guess I'll see you later, guys," Madison said, watching them with narrowed eyes. They seemed awfully edgy. She could've sworn one of the rats was wringing its paws. She just hoped they wouldn't destroy the apartment.

As soon as the door closed behind her, the dam burst.

"Finally!" Butterbean squealed.

"You're not going to believe what happened!" Polo

said, launching herself out of the aquarium. The two blurted out the whole story so quickly that at one point Polo started hyperventilating and had to put her head between her knees.

But it was all worth it. The Coin Man was real. The mission was a success.

"Bravo! Excellent work!" Oscar crowed. "Your plan didn't have the elegance and subtlety of my original plan, but I have to admit, it was effective. So we have a target—Apartment B on the top floor."

"That's the one," Butterbean said, nodding her head. "It was definitely him. He smelled just right."

"Oh boy was he creepy, though," Polo said, shivering. "I didn't like the way he was looking at that girl."

"I didn't like the way he was looking at me!" Butterbean said. "I'm glad we won't be seeing him ever again."

"Yeah, we'll just steer clear of that guy," Polo agreed.

"Um, yes." Oscar frowned. He was having a creeping feeling that the others weren't as clear on the "heist" concept as he'd thought. "We will definitely steer clear of him. After the heist, that is."

"Wait, what?" Butterbean said, cocking her head.

"About that," Marco said. "How does this heisting work, exactly?" He shifted uncomfortably. He hadn't seen a lot of the crime-type shows that Oscar had seen. He was feeling like he and Polo were at a severe disadvantage, heist-wise.

"Well, he's got the coins, so he's the target of our heist," Oscar explained.

Butterbean's head cocked ever farther to the right.

"This is how it works. Now that we've identified the Coin Man, we'll do some surveillance," Oscar said, pacing back and forth across the coffee table like he was teaching Heisting 101. "We'll locate his coins, and then we'll set the heist in motion. Don't worry, I'll plan all that. Right now, you'll just need to do some legwork."

"Oh, okay," Marco said uncertainly. He'd heard of legwork. Mrs. Food did legwork every Wednesday and Friday. He thought his legs were in decent shape already, but he was willing to put in a couple of workouts for the cause. He was pretty good on the wheel.

Polo still wasn't convinced. "But me and Butterbean, we already did our part, right? So we're done?"

"You did excellent work, yes," Oscar said, shifting his wings. He didn't like how suspicious Polo was looking. He definitely should've explained heisting earlier. "But this is just the beginning. We need more information to plan the heist. And then we'll need everyone to pitch in on heist day."

Walt rolled her eyes. The last thing they needed

was a rat mutiny. And Walt didn't think that anyone in the history of heists had ever called it "heist day."

She nudged Oscar to the side. "What Oscar's trying to say is that we can't get the information without you. How many coins there are, where they're hidden—that kind of thing. You follow?"

"Sure," Polo said uncertainly. She absolutely did not follow.

"Follow where?" Marco asked.

Walt sighed. "We need a couple of inside men. Rats. A couple of inside rats."

"Well, yeah, we're inside rats," Marco said. He hadn't met any outside rats. He'd heard about them, though.

"They want you to go in, I think," Butterbean explained. "Inside that creepy guy's apartment. Right, Walt?"

"Right." Walt twitched her tail impatiently.

Polo's nose turned bright pink. "You want us to do WHAT? Are you kidding me? You didn't SEE that guy!"

"I know, he's creepy. We don't want you around that guy," Walt said, holding up her paws defensively. She hadn't realized rats could get so jumpy. "Just scope out the apartment, okay? That's all we want you to do. Just take a look around."

"We can do that," Marco said. "Right, Polo?"

"That guy eats rats like me for LUNCH!" Polo gasped.

"He won't even know you're there!" Walt promised.

"We'll make sure he's gone. Just a quick look. That's all we're asking," Oscar said. "I'd do it myself, but you're the only ones who can fit under the door."

Polo stared at the carpet. That was true. Oscar would never be able to fit under a door. Rats were made for that kind of thing. It was practically the reason they'd been invented.

"We can do this, Polo," Marco said, patting her on the shoulder. "You didn't see yourself on TV. You were amazing! Once you hid under that plant, nobody even knew you were there!"

"Really?" Polo looked up. "You watched me on TV?"

Marco blushed. "Yeah, you looked really good, too. Plus with that button, you looked all glamorous, like a star! Next time we'll tape it." He shot Oscar a look. "We didn't have it set up right this time."

"Well. If he won't be there . . ." Polo looked at Oscar. "What do we have to do?"

"We'll watch on the surveillance cameras until the man leaves the building. That'll be your cue," Oscar said.

Walt nodded. "I've got the door set up so we can

come and go. I'll carry you up on my back. Then just sneak inside, find the coins, and get out of there. If he comes back before you're done, forget the coins and skedaddle. Then report back."

Marco bobbed up and down on the balls of his feet. "Got it. Go, scope, skedaddle!"

"Got it." Polo let out a breath she didn't know she'd been holding. "We don't go until he's gone." She turned to Marco. "You didn't see him. He was scary."

Marco nodded as he bobbed. "We'll be careful. We'll be totally invisible, like ghosts, or superspies." He turned to Oscar. "I like this plan. It'll give me a chance to get some more legwork done." He jogged off, doing a lap around the sofa, punching the air as he went.

Oscar looked at Walt, eyebrows raised. "Legwork?"

"Don't tell him," Walt said under her breath.

⅄⅂⅄⅄⅂⅄⅄⅂⅄⅂⅂⅄⅂⅂⅄⅄

It took three hours for the man in the penthouse apartment to leave the building.

Since only Butterbean and Polo had actually seen the guy, they were the ones on surveillance duty. And they figured out one problem pretty quickly—blue eyes don't show up on fuzzy black-and-white surveillance footage.

"Is that him?" Polo whispered early on. A light-haired man was leaving the elevator in the lobby.

Butterbean leaned forward, nose hovering in front of the screen. "I don't think so. I think that's Stinky Sweat Socks on three."

"Are you sure?" Polo said, watching the man disappear off the edge of the screen.

"Maybe?"

Polo shrugged. "Okay." Maybe would have to be good enough. Better to keep waiting than get it wrong.

After three more false IDs (Guy Who Smokes Cigars, Guy Who Yells at the Doorman, and Mechanic Guy) the Coin Man appeared. And once they'd seen him, there was no question. Even the way he moved across the screen sent chills down Polo's back.

"Okay, you're right—he's creepy," Marco said as they watched the blurry footage of the guy leaving the building. "Look, even the doorman guy doesn't like him."

"Wow, you're right," Butterbean said, pressing her nose against the Television again, leaving a smeary streak behind. "Mr. Doorman talks to EVERYONE, and he didn't say a word to that guy. He just held the door and stepped back."

"Bad news," Polo said, shivering.

"Right," Walt said, standing up. Getting creeped

out wasn't going to do them any good. And Walt was starting to think it was contagious. "Let's get going. Now, you know the signal if he comes back?"

"Howl into the elevator shaft and hope you hear it," Butterbean said solemnly.

"Fly outside, locate his apartment, and peck on the windows," Oscar said.

"Good." Walt nodded. "Hopefully, it won't come to that. I'll be out in the hallway, so I should be able to make a commotion on my own. But as we've seen," she said, shooting a side glance at Oscar, "it's good to have backup plans."

Oscar clicked his beak and then nodded. "Well, better get going," he said, shooing the rats toward the door with his wings. "Hustle. Time's a-wasting."

"Polo? Marco? Climb up." Walt settled down on her haunches and waited as they scrambled onto her back. She tried not to wince as their claws dug into her sides.

"Not so fun, is it?" Butterbean said gloomily.

"It's fine," Walt said through gritted teeth. "Ready, rats? Let's go." She stood up, trying not to jostle the rats too much.

"Whooaaa WHOOOAAAAA," Marco shrieked, letting go of Walt's back and waving his hands in the air like he was on a roller coaster.

"Not the time, Marco," Polo said.

"WHOOOAAAA . . . what? Okay, sorry." Marco put his hands back down and held on to Walt's fur. "Just trying to lighten the mood."

"Well, don't," Polo said sternly. Then she winked. "We can goof around on the way back. AFTER we've found the loot."

Marco grinned. "Got it. Let's go!"

Walt rolled her eyes and slinked carefully to the door. "Oscar?"

Oscar flew over to the door and landed on the handle, jumping up and down just enough to jostle the door open. "Be careful."

Walt took a deep breath and stepped out into the hallway.

The trip up to the top floor was supposed to be the easy part of the plan, but waiting for the Coin Man to leave had put them right into the elevator rush hour. It took them three tries before they got an empty elevator. (Luckily, they went unseen by one teenager wearing headphones, two women looking at their phones, and an old man examining his mail.)

"The trip down may be even trickier," Walt said as she crept into the elevator.

"We'll worry about that later," Marco said. "After all, if the man comes back before we're done, we might not even need to go back down!"

"Geez, Marco!" Polo scrambled onto Walt's head and pushed the top-floor button.

"What? I just mean if he finds us, we could be dead!" Marco scooched back to make room as Polo slid back down onto Walt's back.

"GEEZ! I know what you mean!"

"Guys, seriously?" Walt hissed, watching the floor numbers light up. It was kind of mesmerizing, actually.

"Ninth floor," the elevator voice said as the doors opened.

Walt peered out of the elevator. They could hear muffled noises coming from one of the apartments, but otherwise the hallway seemed deserted. Walt raised an eyebrow at Polo.

Polo shook her head. "Not the one with the noises. It's this one." She pointed at the Coin Man's apartment, trying not to shudder. She could practically still see him in the doorway, looming over the girl and Butterbean.

Without a word, Walt crept out of the elevator, keeping low to the ground. The door closed behind them.

There was no going back.

Walt slunk over to the Coin Man's door, her ears moving as she listened for any sounds from inside. Finally she nodded.

"It's clear. But we should hurry. Get in and get out." Walt had thought most of the "creepy" talk earlier had been silliness, but there was something about that apartment. The hairs on the back of her neck were starting to prickle. "I'll keep watch."

"Got it," Polo said, sliding off Walt's back.

"You can count on us," Marco said. "We'll be super thorough. We're going to split the apartment into zones to search, just like humans do when they're searching a field for a body."

"Geez, Marco!" Polo squeaked. "What have you been watching?"

"What? You can count on us to be thorough, that's all I'm saying!" Marco said defensively. He patted Polo on the shoulder. "Why don't I go first?"

Polo considered for less than half a second. There was no way she was going first. "Yep, sounds good. You first. Get a move on."

Marco nodded solemnly. "Okay. See you on the other side."

After an elaborate show of examining the gap, he lay down on the floor and started crawling into the apartment.

Marco stopped.

"What are you doing?" Polo leaned over and called to Marco, who was halfway under the door, butt high in the air.

"Um. Nothing," Marco said, backing out again. "I just want to try it a different way. I'll back into it. I think it'll be better. For surveillance purposes, I mean."

"Butt first?" Polo said. "Is that a good idea?"

"Yeah, I think it'll be better," Marco said, wriggling his butt under the door and starting to crawl backward.

Marco stopped.

"What is it this time?" Polo asked. Marco's arms were squished forward in a weird way. Polo didn't think they were squished like that for surveillance purposes.

Marco cleared his throat. "Um. My . . . um. My waistline seems to be a little large."

"Well, suck it in!" Polo said, clapping her hands. "Squeeze in there! We're rats—this is what we do!"

"Okay, yes," Marco said, taking a deep breath and wiggling his butt backward. He made it a little farther, up to the bottom of his rib cage. "Um. Polo? No good," he said, his voice a thin squeak. "And now I think I'm stuck."

"Oh, sheesh," Polo grumbled, grabbing Marco by

the paws and dragging him out as he held his breath. "I'll go first, then. But I'm not going butt first."

Polo smoothed her side fur, flattened herself on the floor, and started to crawl under the door. When she hit hip level, she stopped too.

"Problem?" Marco said, looking at Polo's struggling hind legs and tail. They didn't seem to be moving forward anymore.

"Um," Polo said. "Problem."

"Is it your waistline?"

"Um. I think it might be." Polo stopped struggling. "Pull me back out?"

"Sure." Marco grabbed hold of Polo's tail and started tugging. "Hey, Walt? Come here!"

"What's the problem?" Walt came over, eyes still scanning the hallway. Polo was definitely right, this place gave her the creeps.

Marco leaned on Polo's butt and tried to look casual. "What was that you were saying about backup plans?"

– 9 –

"SO WE HAVE A NEW PLAN," WALT SAID AS SHE stalked into the room, taking Butterbean and Oscar by surprise. Oscar snapped his beak shut. It was a little irritating, to be honest, all this changing of his plans.

"What was wrong with the old plan?" Butterbean said, watching as Polo and Marco slid off Walt's back.

Walt shrugged. "The gap under the door is too narrow. It's not rat-sized. We'd need mice. Or maybe snakes. Anyway, that's not important. We've got a better idea."

"Okay," Butterbean agreed. She didn't even need to know what the better idea was, as long as it didn't involve snakes. She'd never met one, but she'd heard things about them. Word on the street was that they flicked their tongues.

Oscar looked thoughtful. "Hmm. Yes. I should have measured the gap." He turned to the rats and bowed his head slightly. "I'm sorry, Marco, Polo. That was a lapse on my part. It was thoughtless of me." Oscar hated to admit it, but the gap size hadn't even crossed his mind, not even once. He'd just assumed that rats were squishy enough that they would have no problem. He didn't actually know that much about rats, now that he thought about it.

"Yeah, it's fine," Marco said, touching his waist. "We should probably go a little easier on the sunflower seeds."

"It was the gap, not you," Walt said dismissively. "You're fine. Now for the new plan—I'm thinking vents."

"What vents?" Butterbean asked.

"Up there," Walt said, nodding up at the air vents near the ceiling. "If I'm right, those vents connect all the apartments in the building. Most of them are up high like those, but I thought we could just use this one." Walt walked over to the sofa and pointed behind it. A small vent was in the baseboard underneath the window.

"A behind-the-sofa vent?" Butterbean said, shocked. How could she have never noticed that before? Her ball had gone back there a thousand times at least. "Who would've expected that?"

"Exactly. Plus, this one's a little special." Walt reached out and swatted at the vent cover. It fell forward with a thump. "I've been working on the screws on this baby for months. Never know when you'll need a good hiding place, you know?"

Oscar whistled in appreciation. "Nice job." He peered into the vent. "And floor level is much easier for me, with my bad back. So this goes . . ."

"To the side, and then up. It connects to the ceiling vents. It's our ticket to the whole building."

Oscar stood up. "And you didn't share this earlier because . . . ?"

"A cat likes to have some secrets, Oscar," Walt sniffed. "I didn't know it would be necessary." She reached into the vent and pulled out a small catnip mouse. "I'll just take this back for now."

"Well, we can definitely fit in there, right, Polo?" Marco said, marching up to the vent and crawling inside. "Oh yeah, this should be a piece of cake. We can climb like nobody's business."

Polo nodded in agreement. "This looks a lot better. So we go how many floors up?"

"Five," Walt said. "Butterbean, can you explain the building layout?"

"Okay, this is how it is," Butterbean said, hunkering down on her haunches. "Most floors have four apartments, right? Well, we're a D apartment, but there are only two on that top floor, and the Coin Man is in B. So I think that means that he's above us."

Walt nodded. "That makes sense. So you'll just have to go straight up. If you're not sure, just look out of the vent grates into the apartments—that should help you get your bearings."

"Got it." Polo smacked her hands together. "Who's in the apartments on eight? Just in case we get confused about what floor we're on?"

"Based on the smells, I'd say Apartment A is the Patchouli Family, Apartment B is Biscuit, Apartment C is the weird pretzely apartment, and Apartment D is Axe Body Spray." Butterbean thumped her tail. "Got it?"

"Wait a minute. I thought Biscuit was on the second floor?" Walt frowned.

"Different Biscuit," Polo said knowingly.

Butterbean patted Walt's paw. "This building has a LOT of Biscuits."

"So we're all set, right?" Polo said. Hopefully, the apartments would be stinky enough that Butterbean's descriptions would help.

"Should we go now?" Marco said, bobbing up and

down inside the vent. The metal on the bottom was making small booming noises, and it made him feel better. He really wanted to put the whole door episode behind him. His ribs were still a little sore.

"Yes, go. Before the girl comes back to walk Bean," Walt said. "We'll try to cover for you if you're not back in time. But hurry."

"Consider it done," Polo said, crawling into the vent after Marco. "This should be a snap. Up, up, and away!"

"WHOOHOOO," Marco shrieked, his voice echoing as he went.

"Marco! Not the time!" Polo's voice could be heard disappearing down the vent.

"Do you think this'll work?" Oscar said, tilting his head toward Walt as the rats' voices faded away.

"Why not?" Walt shrugged. "They're rats. Rats love vents. What could go wrong?"

Marco and Polo were lost. They'd started out taking only the up vents, like Butterbean had suggested. But some of the sideways vents looked pretty interesting, so they decided to take one quick detour. And then another one. And now they were staring through a grate at Bob the maintenance guy.

"I think he's making dinner," Marco whispered, peering out of the grate.

"Did you know he lived here?" Polo whispered. "I thought he lived someplace else. He lives at his work!"

"It smells spicy. Is that spaghetti sauce?" Marco pressed his eye against the grate opening for a better view.

Bob was wearing an apron and whistling to himself while he stirred a pot on the stove. It did smell spicy. Polo craned her neck down to get a closer look.

"I don't know. Could be? Maybe it's soup. It's hard to see." She examined it for a second and then straightened up, smacking Marco on the shoulder. "What are we doing? That's not important! We've got to focus."

"But it's Bob! In his apartment!" Marco said.

"Exactly!" Polo crossed her arms. "Butterbean didn't say anything about Bob, so we're obviously not on the right floor. We might not even be on the right side of the building! We shouldn't have taken that last turn!"

"But it smelled like corn chips!" Marco wailed. "I just wanted a taste!"

"Well, yes, me too," Polo admitted. Corn chips were hard to pass up. "But we need to forget Bob, find an up vent, and get back to work."

"Shhh!" Marco said, putting his hand over Polo's

mouth. They'd kind of forgotten about the whole "being quiet" aspect of surveillance.

"BOB," he mouthed.

Bob had stopped humming.

The rats peered back down through the grate. Bob hadn't just stopped humming. He'd stopped stirring. And he was staring up at them. He was looking right into their eyes.

"Oh, that can't be good," Polo said.

"Whaa—" Bob yelped, dropping his wooden spoon and spattering sauce everywhere. "RATS!"

"I was right. It is spaghetti sauce," Marco smirked.

"Who cares! RUN!" Polo said, grabbing Marco by the shoulder and dashing back down the vent just as Bob's hand smacked across the grate.

"AAAAAHHHHH," Marco shrieked, running after Polo.

"Up! Up! Look for an up vent!" Polo yelled, craning her neck to look at the ceiling. She could hear Bob tugging at the grate. She didn't think he'd be able to reach them, but she didn't want to take that chance.

"There!" Marco pointed. A small up vent was in the corner just a few feet away. "There it is!"

Marco and Polo leaped into the vent just as the grate in Bob's apartment was wrenched off. They crawled up, slipping on the slick metal as they went, not even looking back until they were sure they were safely on the next floor. Then they collapsed in relief.

"Do you think he recognized us?" Polo asked, panting.

"I sure hope not. We do have very distinctive faces, though." Marco ran his hand over his muzzle. "We'll find out soon enough, I guess."

"We've got to stop stalling and get to the top. I can't even tell what floor we're on." Polo sat up and looked around.

"Maybe we could ask him?" Marco said, looking over her shoulder.

"Him who?" Polo turned around and gasped.

A strange rat was crouching in the corner of their vent.

"Who's that?" she squealed. "And what is he doing in our vent?"

"YOUR vent?" the rat squeaked uncertainly. Then he raised himself to his full height. "Excuse me, ma'am, but this is MY vent."

Polo blinked. "Of course. Your vent. We're just passing through. Don't mind us." She knew she'd started to babble. This must be one of those outdoor rats she'd heard about. Not a pet. A WILD rat. She didn't know what to expect from a wild rat. Wild rats were crazy. They'd do anything.

"Yeah, we'll just be going. Sorry about that," Marco said, scrambling to his feet and pulling Polo up with him.

"Not so fast," the Wild Rat said, taking a step toward them.

"We don't want any trouble—" Polo started, but the Wild Rat cut her off.

"Wait a minute . . ." the rat said, squinting at them closely. He took another step closer. "Wait just a minute. Are you . . . are you two PETS?"

Marco and Polo exchanged a worried glance. They didn't know whether yes was the right answer or the wrong answer. And they sure didn't want to give the wrong answer.

"Well, um," Marco started, but he never got to finish.

"You are! You're pets!" the Wild Rat interrupted, hopping up and down. "Me too! I was a pet too!"

"You were?" Polo said uncertainly. "That's great!"

"Isn't it? I was a pet on the second floor! Or I was until one of the children in my household squeezed my middle a bit too hard. Then I decided to take to the vents. It's so nice to meet a fellow pet!" He clasped his hands in front of him and gazed at them with moist eyes. "So tell me. Do they still have that seed mix with the sunflower seeds and corn? I used to love that."

"Um. Yes, that's still pretty much the standard," Marco said.

"Of course, it's a classic." The rat stared at them happily. "And the wheel? I can tell you work out. Is that still the exercise equipment of choice? How I did love a good run on the wheel."

"Um, yes. We use the wheel almost every night," Polo said.

"Nothing better to keep the human family awake, am I right?" the Wild Rat said, nudging Marco in the ribs with his elbow. "But how rude of me, let me introduce myself. My name is Wallace. My pet name was Fuzzy, but you know how that is. I go by Wallace in the vents."

"I'm Marco, and this is Polo," Marco said, extending a hand, which Wallace grabbed and immediately started to shake enthusiastically. "Are there a lot of rats in the vents?"

Wallace made a sad face. "No, not too many. Just me, actually, although I have a nice circle of friends who live out back in the loading dock. Are you all looking to relocate?"

Polo and Marco exchanged a nervous glance. "Not exactly. But our circumstances may be changing, so . . ." Polo hesitated. She wasn't sure how much she should confide in Wallace. She didn't really want to tell him about Mrs. Food, or the coin guy.

"Look, it's like this," Marco said. He wasn't the least bit worried about confiding. "Our living situation is a little iffy right now, so we're treasure hunting. Hoping to be independently wealthy, if you know what I mean. We've got a lead on some treasure, and we're going to scope it out right now, in fact."

"Way to go, Marco," Polo muttered. Sometimes he just couldn't keep his mouth shut.

Wallace looked skeptical. "Treasure? In the vents? I haven't seen it."

"Not in the vents, in one of the apartments," Marco boasted. "We're on a mission, see."

"Oh," Wallace said. "That sounds nice."

Polo rolled her eyes. "The treasure may not even exist, okay? But the problem is that we're lost. Can you help us find the apartment?"

Wallace shrugged. "I could probably help. What floor is it? You're in the seventh-floor vents at the moment. That's my preferred floor. Primo accommodations on Floor Seven."

"It's not seven. It's the top floor. Apartment B," Polo said.

Wallace went pale. Polo could actually see the blood drain out of his face as she spoke. He cleared his throat. "Apartment B?"

"That's right," Polo said. "On the top floor. Do you know it?"

"Oh no. No no no. No indeed no, I don't go there. Not to that apartment. Have you SEEN that man who lives there?" Wallace took a few steps back. "If there's treasure in that apartment, you should leave it alone. I think you should just go home. Or if your living situation changes, live here in the vents with me! There's plenty of room. Floor Five seems quite nice." Wallace clenched his hands together and leaned forward. "I would stay away from that apartment. I really would."

Marco and Polo exchanged a worried glance.

"That's the thing," Marco said. "We really can't. We need to at least look inside."

"It's important," Polo explained. "We'll be careful."

Wallace clenched his jaw and sighed. "Okay. I can show you the way. But I won't go to that floor with you. You're on your own there."

"That would be fine," Polo said. The fur on the back of her neck prickled uncomfortably. And she'd thought the guy was creepy enough before Wallace freaked out. She was starting to hate Oscar's ideas.

"It's this way," Wallace said, climbing into an up vent that was partially concealed by a pipe.

Marco and Polo followed silently. If this rat who had started a new life in the wild was too afraid to go to the Coin Man's apartment, what the heck were they doing?

Wallace pulled Polo and Marco up after him into the eighth-floor vents. Then he patted Polo on the shoulder. "Remember, you always have a home in the vents. And if you wanted to bring some snacks when you moved in, that would be good too. I have some perfect storage spots for seeds and whatnot."

"We'll bring you some corn and sunflower seeds either way," Marco said. "We owe you one."

"Just be careful," Wallace said. "Good luck." He

grabbed Marco by the hand and clasped it tightly. Then he scurried away without another word.

Marco turned to Polo. "So, should we just go on up?"

Polo shook her head as she looked around. "Let's look into some of the apartments first. Get our bearings. I don't want to make any more mistakes."

She scurried down to the apartment grate at the end of the vent. "According to Butterbean this should be . . . what?"

Marco frowned as he thought. "Butterbean said that one apartment on this side smelled weird and pretzely, and one smelled like Axe Body Spray."

Polo rolled her eyes. "Axe Body Spray? I'll take a look. Catch me if the smell knocks me out." She sniffed cautiously at the grate. "Not the Axe Body Spray one."

She peeked up into the vent. "Huh. It does smell kind of empty and pretzelish. I wonder who—HEY!" Polo's whiskers bristled, and her eyes widened. "Marco! It's the girl!"

Marco turned to look so quickly that he bruised his nose on the grate. "OUR girl? She lives in this one?"

They pressed their faces to the grate to get a closer look. Madison's pink backpack was on the kitchen table, and she was sitting alone reading a book.

"Why don't I smell other people there?" Polo said. "Heck, I barely smell her."

"Your nose isn't as good as Butterbean's, I guess. It makes sense that the girl lives somewhere, though, right? Why not here? Bob lives here. In the building, I mean."

Polo shook her head as she watched Madison read. "It feels wrong. Something is wrong. I don't like this."

Marco gasped. "Oh man. You're right something is wrong. Look at her."

Madison had stopped reading. She put her book down on the table and stood up. Then she picked up her jacket and a set of keys hanging by the door.

"What?" Polo said, watching Madison put her shoes on. "What's so wrong?"

"We've taken too long," Marco said, pointing at Madison. "She's leaving. Don't you see?"

He grabbed Polo by both shoulders.

"She's leaving to go take care of us."

– 10 –

"IT'LL BE FINE, RIGHT?" POLO LEAPED LIKE a rat Olympic high jumper into the up vent. "The others will cover for us. The girl will never suspect that we're gone."

"Maybe Walt will pretend she ate us. I'd buy that," Marco said, pulling himself up into the vent after her.

"Walt would never eat us," Polo scoffed.

"Maybe not before. But NOW? If we've messed this up, she'll be super mad. We need to hurry!" Marco looked wildly around the top-floor vent. He didn't know how Wallace could tell them all apart. "Is it that one?" He pointed to a shadowy grate a few feet away.

"I think so," Polo said. "Now calm down. We have

to do this right. It won't do us any good to panic."
She edged toward the grate. She could practically feel
the Coin Man waiting for her. She braced herself and
nodded at Marco. "Let's go."

The elevator ding in the hallway took Walt, Oscar,
and Butterbean by surprise. Walt was taking care of
a little personal hygiene, Oscar was having a millet
snack, and Butterbean was playing with a piece of fluff
on the floor. None of them expected Madison to come
back so soon. Butterbean sat up so quickly that she
inhaled her fluff. "Madison?" she coughed.

Walt stopped midlick, her ears swiveling toward
the door.

"Oh no," Butterbean gasped.

"Urk," Oscar choked, spitting out a flurry of millet
shells.

"It can't be," Walt said. Surely it was someone for
some other apartment. "It can't be time yet."

"I do need to pee," Butterbean said. She hadn't
wanted to mention it before, but it was true.

A key turned in the lock. The three stared at one
another in horror.

"Quick. Distractions. Don't let her see they're
gone," Oscar said, flying around his cage and

hopping on the perch. "Do whatever it takes!"

The door opened, and Madison stepped inside smiling. "Hey, you guys!" she said brightly.

"Butterbean, go," Walt said under her breath. Butterbean nodded and launched herself at Madison.

"How's it—oof!" Madison was abruptly cut off by the small furry dog slamming into her kneecaps. "HEY!"

"OUT OUT, OH PLEASE TAKE ME OUT OUT OUT," Butterbean wailed, jumping up and down.

"That should do it," Walt said softly, hopping up onto the table next to Marco and Polo's empty aquarium. She lounged casually in front of it, trying to hide the lack of occupants from view.

"Okay, sure, little guy, just give me a second," Madison said, laughing and trying to dodge Butterbean's wild jumps in the air. "Just let me check on the others real quick. Then we'll go."

"OH NO, NO TIME, NEED TO PEE, PLEASE PLEASE," Butterbean yelped, doing her best need-to-pee dance. Oscar watched, impressed. She was really outdoing herself.

Madison patted at Butterbean absently and made her way over to Oscar's cage. "Everything okay, bird?"

"Fine," Oscar said in his human voice.

"Oh." Madison reeled back, shocked. "Well, good." Oscar eyed her carefully.

Butterbean slowed her pee dance down to a lazy shuffle and frowned at Madison. "I should totally pee on the floor. She would deserve it."

"Please don't, Bean," Walt said, draping herself over the aquarium dramatically. "You're doing great."

"It's like she doesn't even understand urgency," Butterbean lamented, doing a jig around the entryway.

"And how are you?" Madison said, walking over to Walt. "Are you okay? You look . . . strange?"

Walt blinked at her.

"And how are your little friends?" Madison said, bending down to peer inside the aquarium.

"EMERGENCY! EMERGENCY!" Oscar screeched. "Distraction, Walt!"

Walt scanned the area for options. A water glass that Mrs. Food had left on the table was standing nearby. Walt reached out slowly and put a paw on it.

Madison stopped immediately. "Oh no. Don't do that."

Walt meowed and pushed the glass an inch forward.

"Good kitty. Just leave the glass alone." Madison stepped forward, her hands outstretched.

Walt pushed the glass closer to the edge of the table, paused, and then shoved it slowly off the edge.

"No!" Madison lunged forward and caught the glass in midair. "Whew! Silly cat!"

She carried the glass into the kitchen and put it in the sink. Then she grabbed Butterbean's leash and came back to the living room. "Good grief, what's with you guys today?"

She clipped the leash onto Butterbean's collar and opened the door.

Butterbean smirked as she trotted out of the house. "About time!"

"Thank goodness," Oscar said, slumping down on his perch. "We did it."

"For now," Walt said, turning to look at the vent.

"But this doesn't make sense." Polo peered through the dusty grate. "This is the apartment with the treasure? This place is so . . . BORING."

"Right? Where are the piles of jewels? Where's all the gold?" Marco looked around at the beige living room. He'd expected walls encrusted with gems, or maybe some kind of seedy criminal lair. Not boring tweed sofas and vinyl chairs.

Polo scurried down the vent to the next grate along the line. Standing on her hind legs, she quickly peered inside. It was a standard bedroom, nothing flashy or special. Definitely not a treasure lair. "Beige," she muttered. "Everything is beige."

"Weird. It's not personal AT ALL," Marco said.

"It's like it's all rented." Polo brightened. "Maybe that's it! Maybe this is just a place where they stash their loot!"

"Okay, sure," Marco agreed. "But then where's the loot?"

"I don't know." Polo had never felt so confused. Knowing whose apartment it was, she'd expected cold waves of evil to come from everything inside, but it was all just so ordinary.

Marco pointed down the vent. "There's one more grate. We could try it. But I think it's the—"

"Oh no," Polo squeaked. "Marco, that's the bathroom grate. No thank you. You can check if you want." She rolled her eyes. She'd never heard about treasure stashed in the bathroom.

"I'll just take a quick look-see," Marco said, heading down to the final grate. He stuck his eye up to one of the gaps. He'd hardly taken a look when he squeaked and jumped back. "Polo! It's—there's someone here! Look!"

Polo rushed to the grate and then hung back. "I can't look!"

"Why not?"

"They're in the bathroom!"

"Just look! It's not embarrassing. And it's NOT the creepy guy! No blue eyes!"

Polo covered her eyes (in case the person in the bathroom needed a little privacy), but as soon as she took a peek, she dropped her hands in shock.

"Who's that guy?" she squeaked.

The man at the bathroom sink wasn't the creepy

Coin Man. This guy had shaggy hair and brown eyes, and he was wearing a shiny-looking suit. He didn't seem particularly friendly, but he wasn't giving Polo the heebie-jeebies like the other man had. He didn't look like he'd eat her for lunch.

Marco and Polo pressed their faces to the grate, watching as the shaggy guy dried his hands on his pants and then headed out into the living room.

"Quick, to the other grate!" Marco squealed, hurrying back toward the living room.

"A second guy," Polo said under her breath. "Oh, that's not good."

"No, and what's worse, there's no sign of treasure at all," Marco called over his shoulder.

"Of course not, not in the bathroom," Polo scoffed.

"But, Polo. Maybe Butterbean was wrong?" Marco slumped against the grate. "Oh man, we're going to be living in the vents after all." He ruffled his hands through the fur on his head. "I don't even know if there'll be room for Walt and Butterbean and Oscar. Do you think they can squeeze?"

"Don't be ridiculous. We're not living in the vents," Polo said. At least she hoped not, because the others would absolutely not be able to squeeze. "Butterbean's nose is reliable. Just keep watching."

The shaggy-haired man was looking in the

refrigerator, apparently unhappy with what he saw. He stared inside for a few minutes and finally closed it without getting anything. Then he opened a couple of cabinets, sighed, and closed them again.

"I know that feeling," Marco muttered.

The man took out his phone and started looking at it.

"That's it," Marco said, pushing away from the grate. "There's no point in watching this. We failed. Again. There's nothing we can do."

"We can't give up!" Polo squeaked. "Sure, it's all boring. But it's surveillance! It's supposed to be boring!"

Marco sighed. "I think we were wrong, Polo. I don't think there's any treasure. Maybe it was just the one coin."

Polo clenched her jaw. "What did you want him to do, just pull out the coins and start counting them?" she said. "Pretty unrealistic, Marco. This isn't a movie."

"I expected something!" Marco said, waving his arm in the direction of the grate. "More than this!"

The man in the apartment put down his phone and sighed. Then he opened the cabinet-style end table by the couch and took out a small duffel bag. He hoisted it onto the coffee table, unzipped it, and dumped out a stash of gold coins.

"Holy cow," Polo said in a low voice.

Marco's eyes bugged out as he looked at the pile. "Guess it wasn't so unrealistic after all, huh."

"I guess not." Polo raised her hand for a high five. "Whoohoo!"

"Whoo!" Marco echoed, high-fiving her. "We did it! We found the coins. And boy, there are a LOT of them."

"Tons," Polo said. "Good news for us, right?"

"Right!"

They watched the man counting the gold pieces in front of him. It was strangely soothing. They were so shiny.

Finally Marco shot Polo a sidelong look. "How are we ever going to carry a bag like that?"

Polo didn't answer. She just stared at the pile of coins and the duffel bag that was almost as big as Butterbean.

Walt was trying to look calm, but her tail was twitching wildly. She didn't think she would be able to keep Madison from noticing the aquarium again. It was pretty obvious the rats weren't in it.

"Maybe I could pretend my wing is broken? Do a big show of flapping around?" Oscar said thoughtfully.

He'd done a little acting in his younger days. Maybe it was time to get back to his roots.

"Sure, but what would she do then, take you to the vet?" Walt said. "We don't want that."

"No, true," Oscar said, shuddering. He definitely didn't want to go to the vet. "So no wing. Another hairball?"

"I can try, but I'd rather not." Hairballs were Walt's specialty, but she hated to overuse them.

"We'll keep that as a backup then. As a last resort." Oscar tapped his beak against the bars of his cage. "Should I soil my newspaper?"

"Do you think she'd notice?" Walt asked.

"Hmm. Maybe not," Oscar admitted.

"Still, it's worth a try," Walt said. Marco and Polo had been gone a long time. She'd been so sure they would be back before Butterbean and Madison returned, but now she was afraid they might not come back at all. They didn't really know anything about those vents, after all. Anything could have happened.

The elevator dinged in the hallway.

"The girl?" Oscar asked.

"I think so." Walt took a deep breath and stood up. She took one last glance at the vent. Empty.

"I'm ready to soil as needed," Oscar said.

"Thanks," Walt said as she listened to Butterbean's tags jingling in the hallway. "Here we go."

As the key turned in the lock, Walt heard a loud skittering behind her. Marco and Polo ran out into the living room just as the door started to swing open.

"Rats! Take cover!" Oscar screamed. "It's the girl!"

"Shoot!" Marco squeaked in alarm, immediately bumping into Polo and knocking them both over.

Walt took one look at the slapstick rat routine behind her and made a decision. And as Madison walked in the door with Butterbean, she sprang.

"Whoa!" Madison squealed as Walt hit her full in the chest, knocking her back. "Cat!"

Walt held on with her claws and scaled Madison's chest until she'd reached Madison's shoulders, immediately whipping her tail into Madison's face. "GO GO GO!" Walt meowed as she coiled her body around Madison's head.

"GO!" Marco said, grabbing Polo by the hand and giving her a boost up the table leg. The two scrambled for the aquarium as Madison staggered out of the entryway.

"Should I wrap my leash around her legs?" Butterbean barked excitedly. "That could be fun!"

"We don't want to kill her!" Oscar squawked.

"Oh, okay," Butterbean pouted, sitting down on

the rug. "It's safe now, Walt! They're inside again."

Marco and Polo slid down the water bottle into their cage, flopping into a pile in the cedar chips and pretending to be asleep. It wasn't hard to do. They were both exhausted. The wheel didn't keep them as in shape as they'd thought.

"Sheesh, cat, I'm glad to see you, too, but come on!" Madison managed to scoop Walt off her shoulders and set her down gently on the couch. "Good kitty," she said, patting Walt on the head.

Walt ignored her and started licking her tail.

Madison snorted and turned to the other animals. "Okay, so everybody good, then? Anybody else crazy today? Rats?" Madison peeked into their aquarium. "Rats are good? Bird? Good? Okay then. See you guys." She staggered back toward the door and grabbed for the handle. "Sheesh!"

She scooted through the doorway quickly, like she expected the animals to jump her again, and then she was gone.

Marco rolled over on his back and groaned. Polo popped her head out of the aquarium. "Is it safe? Because oh man, we've got problems."

— 11 —

"WHAT DO YOU MEAN THERE'S ANOTHER GUY?"
Walt said, lashing her tail in frustration. Butterbean
stepped quietly to the side. Walt had already hit her in
the face with it three times. It kind of stung.

"That's what we saw! There's another guy!" Marco
insisted. "He was counting the coins!"

"He's not as creepy as the main guy. But we still
have to get past him, too," Polo pointed out. "That's
TWICE as many guys."

"Not to mention figuring out how we're going to
carry such a HUGE bag of coins. That thing was as big
as Butterbean!" Marco said. "I was thinking Oscar could
grab it, but how could he fly with it? It'd be so heavy!"

"He has a bad back!" Polo said, pointing at Oscar.

"It's not that bad," Oscar said, shifting awkwardly. So he had a few twinges every now and then. It's not like he was totally incapacitated.

"We thought maybe we could pass the coins under the door and drag them down in the elevator," Marco said.

"But we still have to get someone on the inside! And how do we do that? Again, we were thinking Oscar, but how do we get those open?" Polo said, waving her arms at the windows.

"And again, bad back!" Marco squeaked.

Polo slumped against the table leg. "We have a lot of issues to work out."

"Hold on," Walt said, pacing back and forth in front of the Television. "Hold on."

"Okay," Butterbean said uncertainly.

Everyone watched as Walt stalked across the floor, head down, obviously deep in thought.

"Hold on," Walt said again, even though nobody had said anything. The others kept watching.

"Hold on to what?" Butterbean said finally.

"I've got it." Walt sat down on the carpet. "Problem solved. We can do this."

"Wonderful," Oscar said cautiously. "Mind telling us how?"

"I've got a guy," Walt said. "He can help us. He can handle the inside work."

"You've got a guy," Oscar said.

"I've got a guy." Walt lashed her tail in satisfaction.

Oscar opened his mouth and then shut it again. Butterbean cocked her head to the side.

"We'll have to ask him, but if we present it the right way, I think he'll do it," Walt said confidently. "It's perfect."

Butterbean cocked her head even farther to the side.

"You've got a guy," Oscar said again.

Walt nodded.

Butterbean erupted.

"YOU'VE GOT A GUY?" Butterbean lifted off the ground with every word. "WHO ARE YOU? You've got a guy! You've got a secret vent! You have computer skills! THERE ARE RATS AND YOU KNEW! It's like I don't even KNOW you anymore, Walt!"

"The dog has a point," Oscar said dryly.

"Calm down, Bean," Walt said. She'd never seen Butterbean get so worked up. The stress was obviously taking a toll.

"DON'T 'BEAN' ME!" Butterbean yelped. "YOU HAVE A SECRET LIFE."

"Is it Bob?" Marco asked. "Is he your guy?"

Walt blinked. "Bob? No. Why would it be Bob?" The idea that she'd have a secret connection to Bob was more than a little disturbing. What kind of cat did they think she was?

"Just asking. We saw him through the grates. He LIVES here. In the building." Marco's eyes gleamed.

Walt made a face. "No, it's not Bob. I didn't even know he lived here." She was going to have to make a note of that. Apparently, she didn't know the building as well as she thought. "It's a guy upstairs. He lives on eight."

Butterbean gave a sputtering, weird bark. "You have a GUY on EIGHT? There's no GUY on EIGHT. Except for Mr. Axe Body Spray. Is it him?" Little flecks of spit were flying out of her mouth as she barked.

"He's on eight," Walt said calmly, flexing her claws.

Butterbean stared at her for a minute, then turned her back and marched huffily to the door. "Then let's go see him. Right now." She tapped her feet impatiently.

"Butterbean, wait," Oscar said. "We don't know anything about this guy."

"Trust me. He can get this done," Walt said dismissively.

"But who is this person, Walt?" Oscar asked, snapping his beak a few times. "This all seems very strange." He wasn't going to lose control the same way Butterbean had, but Walt's attitude was making him very uncomfortable. She was much more secretive than he had realized. It threw the whole heist situation into a new light. Was she a cat to be trusted?

Walt sighed and sat down. "Okay. Remember when I used to slip out to explore the building?"

Oscar nodded. "Mrs. Food was frantic that you'd get into the elevator."

"Well, I did. And at one point I made some contacts. One contact. This is him."

"And he is?" Oscar said, hopping closer to her. She seemed sincere, but this was a whole new side of Walt.

"They call him the Octopus."

"Because it's like he's got eight arms?" Butterbean scoffed.

"Because he's an octopus," Walt said.

"Right," Butterbean said. "And I'm a poodle."

Walt stalked over to the door. "You want to meet him, Bean? Then fine, let's go. If anyone can help us, he can. And if he can't . . . well, I don't know what we're going to do."

Butterbean looked at Oscar. His shoulders sagged. "Report back what you find out. And please, try not to get caught."

Butterbean nodded. Her tail started to quiver, but she suppressed the impulse to wag. She was going to get to the bottom of Walt's secret life. But more importantly, she was going OUT. WITHOUT A LEASH.

"Bean!" A tiny whisper came from the direction of the aquarium.

Butterbean looked around. Polo was waving her arm and whispering at her in a really hissy, spitty kind of way. "BEAN!"

Butterbean gave Walt a chilly look. "I need a moment." She trotted over to Polo. "What? Do you want to come? I guess we could do the tummy thing again."

Polo shook her head. "Oh heck no. But if you're going to eight . . . you know that weird empty apartment?"

Butterbean nodded. "With the pretzel smell?"

"That's the one." Polo looked around before drawing Butterbean aside. "We looked inside the grate," she whispered. "Madison was there."

Butterbean's eyes widened. "Madison? The girl?"

"Yeah, and there's something wrong there—I just know it. Maybe you could check it out? See what you can smell?" Polo looked uncomfortable. She didn't want to interfere in Madison's life, but she had a big feeling it was something important. "I'm . . . I'm worried."

"She was acting suspicious on our walk, too," Butterbean said, frowning. "I'll see if I can find anything out."

"Good," Polo said. Madison had always been nice to her, giving her the button and all. She didn't like the idea that there was something bad going on there.

"Butterbean?" Walt called from the doorway. "Let's go."

Butterbean gave Polo a significant look. "You can count on me."

Walt and Butterbean sat in the shadows, waiting for an empty elevator. They'd already had to pass up four because of the people inside, and Butterbean was fed up.

"Next one, I'm just going. I don't care if there's somebody inside. I'm a resident. I'm entitled to use the elevator," Butterbean muttered under her breath.

"Keep cool, Bean," Walt said quietly, twitching her tail. Elevator waiting was an art. You had to lose yourself in the stillness of the empty hallway. Butterbean wasn't very good at stillness.

The elevator dinged. "That's it. I'm on this one. It's mine," Butterbean said, standing up.

"Sit down, Bean," Walt said. She really hoped Butterbean wasn't going to blow this. And barging into an occupied elevator? That would be the quickest way to blow it.

The elevator doors opened. An elderly lady wearing a neon track suit and headband was walking in place inside.

"Oh good. One of the power walkers. Coming, Walt?" Butterbean trotted into the elevator without a backward glance, stood up, and pressed the button for eight with her nose. She sat down quietly and looked up at Mrs. Power Walker, her tongue lolling out of the side of her mouth.

"Bean!" Walt meowed, slipping into the elevator just as the doors closed.

Mrs. Power Walker watched Butterbean warily but kept walking in place. "Um. Hello, doggie," she said after a minute.

Butterbean gave a low woof.

"I don't believe this," Walt said, trying to make herself invisible in the corner of the elevator.

"Seventh floor," the elevator voice said as the doors opened.

Mrs. Power Walker gave Butterbean and Walt a quick wave and then power walked out of the elevator at top speed. She seemed disconcerted about something.

"Never do that again," Walt said as the doors closed.

"What? It worked, right? Like she'll say anything," Butterbean said, grinning. She was glad it had been Mrs. Power Walker. She would never admit it to Walt, but if it had been someone else, like Mrs. Hates Dogs on six, she wouldn't have tried it.

"Eighth floor," the elevator voice said.

"Here we go," Walt said, stepping out of the elevator. She crossed down to the far apartment and knocked on the door.

"But that's Mr. Axe Body Spray's apartment. Your guy really is Mr. Axe Body Spray?" Butterbean said in shock. "And you just KNOCK?"

"Roommates," Walt said. "Now quiet."

Butterbean heard a small sound on the other side of the door. It was a strange sound, something she couldn't quite identify. But it made the hair on the back of her neck prickle.

"Chad. Open up. It's Walt," Walt said in a low voice.

The locks in the door slowly started to turn, and the door opened.

Chad stood in the doorway.

Butterbean sat down hard on her haunches. "Holy cow, Walt. You weren't kidding. He really is an octopus."

Chad the octopus sat in the toilet tapping his tentacles against the seat as he listened to Walt explain the Mrs. Food situation. Butterbean couldn't tell from his expression whether he was bored or happy to see them or comatose.

"So that's what we need you to do," Walt said from her perch on the edge of the tub.

"I don't understand why we're in the bathroom," Butterbean said, looking down at the dark blue bathmat. Everything in Chad's apartment looked hip and modern, even the bathroom stuff. And everything reeked of Axe Body Spray.

"Hush, Bean," Walt said under her breath.

"I like it in here," Chad said quietly. "The tile is cool. I can think."

"Okay," Butterbean said. It looked like she was shedding on the mat. She hoped Mr. Axe Body Spray wouldn't notice.

"So, Walt, what's in it for me?" Chad said, splashing quietly. He started counting off on his tentacles. "One, I don't live with your human, so her fall doesn't affect me. Two, I'm not at risk here. Look at this place. I'm set for life. I have everything an octopus could want. Why should I waste my time?"

"Well," Walt started.

"Walt says that you can get out of anything. Or into anything," Butterbean interrupted. "She says that locks can't stop you."

"Walt has a big mouth," Chad said.

"Yeah, no kidding!" Butterbean snorted. "But how is that possible? About the locks, I mean. You live in a tank and hang out in a toilet."

The octopus shrugged. It was like he was doing the wave all by himself.

"Cute friend, Walt. But this isn't convincing me. Why should I help you?"

Walt jumped down onto the bath mat. "Hilarious good times?"

Chad folded his tentacles in front of him.

"And I know where Mrs. Food keeps the sardines."
The octopus seemed to consider. "I'm in."

"So that went well," Butterbean said after Chad closed the door behind them. There had been more haggling, but in the end Chad had seemed enthusiastic about the whole heist idea. Well, as enthusiastic as Butterbean thought Chad could be. He didn't do cartwheels or anything.

"I hope so," Walt said. "I think this is all coming together, Butterbean. I just hope we're moving quickly enough."

"Wait one second—I promised Polo," Butterbean said, stopping at the empty-smelling apartment. Madison's apartment.

Walt rolled her eyes as the elevator dinged. "Bean, there's no time," she muttered, slinking back into the shadows as the elevator doors opened.

Just in time, too. Bob stepped out into the hallway. He was flipping through a stack of papers and heading straight for Madison's apartment.

Butterbean gave a muffled yelp and hid behind a pillar.

Luckily, Bob was too focused on his papers to notice her yelp, or see her tail sticking out into the hallway. (Butterbean was always the first one caught in hide-and-seek.)

He banged loudly on Madison's door.

After a few minutes the chain on the door was pulled back, and Madison opened it a crack. Then she plastered a smile on her face and opened the door slightly wider. Not too wide, though, Butterbean noticed. And that smile was definitely fake.

"Oh, hi, what's up, Mr.—Bob?" Madison said. She looked nervous, like she'd been caught doing something sketchy. Butterbean could smell waves of panic all the way across the hallway.

"Hey, kid, is your aunt here?" Bob said, peering behind her into the apartment. "I need to talk to her about your pet-watching situation."

"Um, no. She's not. She's at work," Madison said, shifting from one foot to the other.

"Huh. I thought she was in what, the navy? Something like that? Weird time to be at work," Bob said, still looking into the apartment.

Madison laughed, but she pulled the door almost shut behind her. "Close. Army. But she's at a meeting. For the army. That kind of meeting. I'll tell her you stopped by."

"Fine, well, just wanted to give you all the heads-up. You won't need to watch those animals much longer.

Their owner woke up, but it doesn't look like she'll be able to live on her own. So those guys are headed for the shelter, probably in a day or so. Also, your aunt needs to fill out these forms so we can pay you. She'll need to sign them."

Madison stared at the papers. "I can't just sign them?"

Bob snorted. "You're a kid. An adult needs to sign. Anyway, tell your aunt I said hi, and I'll stop by later about the papers. And I'll let you know when we need those animals rounded up—we may need your help with that. Okay, later." He turned and headed back to the elevator. It came immediately.

"Great," Madison said, still staring at the stack of papers. After a few moments she quietly closed the door.

Walt shot out of the shadows and streaked over to Butterbean.

"Did you hear that?" Walt said in a low yowl. "Did you hear what he said?"

Butterbean nodded. "I did. Polo is right. There's something wrong there—that girl does not live with her aunt. I don't think there's anyone else living there."

"That's not what I'm talking about, Butterbean!" Walt shrieked. "About Mrs. Food! He said she's not coming back."

"But what does that mean?" Butterbean said. She'd heard Bob, but she didn't want to think about what he'd said. Or what it meant. Especially now that Walt was totally losing it. That was never a good sign.

"I'll tell you what it means," Walt said in a low voice. "Heist day is NOW."

− 12 −

"WALT, CALM DOWN!" OSCAR SAID. EVER SINCE she'd gotten back with Butterbean, Walt had been literally bouncing off the walls. Oscar flew to a safe perch on the bookshelf as Walt sideswiped his cage. "Walt, be rational. We can't do the heist right now. We're not set up for it!"

"But we don't have time to wait!" Walt said, leaping from the chair to the couch. "We've got to move! Butterbean, tell them!"

Butterbean sat awkwardly on the rug. She didn't seem bothered by Walt's flight pattern. "It's true. We heard Bob talking to Madison. He said Mrs. Food can't come live here anymore. He used the *S* word."

She looked around significantly. Marco looked at Polo and shrugged. He knew lots of *S* words.

"Shelter," Butterbean said. "He said we're going to a shelter."

"Oh, that's not good," Polo said. She'd seen the commercials on TV, and the animals always looked really sad. She didn't think the shelter was a real option for her or for Marco, though. She hadn't ever heard about rescue rats. No, it would be the vents for them.

"The point is, they're coming for us. If we don't move now, it's all over," Walt said, temporarily pausing on the back of the couch.

Oscar flew over and landed on the cushion beside her. "Walt, think rationally. Look outside."

Walt turned and looked at the window. It was dark.

"It's nighttime," Oscar said. "We can't move now. People will be in their apartments. They'll notice if we try to heist now. During the day, neighbors might overlook a random dog or cat or—"

"Octopus," Butterbean piped up.

"Octopus," Oscar agreed. Then he frowned. "The point is, this time, we need to stick to our plan."

"But Bob said . . ." Walt said.

"Bob." Oscar gave a harsh laugh. "Bob isn't going to do anything until his paperwork is done, and who knows how long that will take. We'll stick to the plan.

We'll make our preparations tonight, as planned, wait until the Coin Man leaves, as planned, and then we move. As planned. We'll be swimming in gold coins and long gone before Bob even remembers we're here."

Walt shook her head. "I don't know, Oscar. He said shelter." Walt had been in a shelter as a kitten. She didn't want to go back.

"There's always Plan B, right, Marco?" Polo piped up. "If we need it."

"Plan B? What's Plan B?" Walt said suspiciously.

"Yes, what's Plan B?" Oscar said, eyeing the rats. He didn't like the way they were always coming up with their own plans. Or the way they were always calling them Plan B. It was confusing. And besides, there was only one mastermind of this organization, and they were not it.

"What she means is, there's always the vents," Marco said. "We can stay there temporarily, if we need to." He nudged Polo in the side. "Me and Polo, we know a guy."

"That's right!" Polo squeaked. "We know a guy!"

Walt lifted a lip in an attempt at a smile. She didn't think the vents sounded like a better option.

Oscar sniffed. There was no way he was going to be a vent bird. He'd rather find a tree somewhere and try his luck in the park. But there was no need to tell the rats that, not when they were so close to stealing the treasure. "Yes. Well, it's good to have a Plan B. And in the meantime, Walt, I think we have something to show you that may convince you!" Oscar nudged Walt awkwardly with his wing.

"Show her! Show her!" Polo and Marco cheered, jumping up and down.

"What? Show her what?" Butterbean barked, jumping up and down too. It was easy to get caught up in the excitement. She couldn't bounce off the walls as well as Walt, but she was pretty good at up and down.

"Wait here." Oscar flew into the kitchen. There were a couple of muffled thumps, followed by what sounded like some low-level grumbling. Then they heard the sound of loudly flapping wings.

"What is it? WHAT IS IT?" Butterbean shrieked, thumping her tail on the floor. This was the most exciting week ever in the history of the apartment.

Suddenly Oscar appeared, dramatically framed in the doorway. He hovered for a second, as if he was posing, with Mrs. Food's large handbag hanging from his claws.

"Look! I'm—" Oscar squawked before suddenly dropping a few inches. He flapped his wings awkwardly and rose back up to the center of the doorway. "Bag! See?" he said quickly, maintaining his altitude this time.

"WHOOOHOO!" Marco and Polo cheered, raising their tiny fists in the air.

Oscar flew into the middle of the living room and dropped the handbag onto the coffee table with a thunk, narrowly missing the rat cheering section.

"We were practicing!" Marco said.

"He can carry the bag! " Polo added.

"Even with his bad back!" Marco said.

Oscar leaned up against the handbag. "I should be able to carry the bag out of the apartment, if it's only for a few minutes."

"See? The plan will work!" Polo said.

"We'll be just like a real outlaw gang," Marco cheered. "Ooh! We need a name! Something catchy. How about the Coin Robbers? Or Fourth-Floor Bandits?"

"Since we live in the Strathmore building, what about the Strathmore Five?" Polo suggested.

"Or Strathmore Six if we include the octopus." Marco didn't want to leave Chad out. He didn't want any hard feelings in the outlaw gang.

"Done!" Polo cheered. "Six sounds better anyway." The rats high-fived each other.

"Hmm," Walt sniffed, then jumped over and nosed the handbag. "Hmm," she said again, grudgingly. "That's something, at least."

"It's more than something," Oscar said huffily. "It's everything. All we have to do is be patient, and we'll be set. Independently wealthy. Set for life."

"Set for life," Butterbean echoed.

"Strathmore Six, set for life!" Polo and Marco cheered.

Walt sighed. "Okay. Set for life. Now let's get ready."

When Madison arrived the next morning, the tension in the apartment was so thick that Oscar was surprised she didn't notice. But she didn't. In fact, she didn't seem to notice much of anything.

"Hi, guys. What's up?" she said as she walked in, making a beeline for the dining room table. Butterbean had to do some fancy footwork to avoid getting stepped on, and Madison didn't even blink.

She had the bunch of papers in her hands, and all of her attention seemed to be focused on them.

"We're the Strathmore Six now," Butterbean said. Madison automatically patted her on the head as she went by.

"I can probably just sign them, right?" she said to Marco and Polo absently as she poured food into their cage.

"Sure?" Polo said, trying to be agreeable. It sounded like a legal question, and Polo wasn't really confident about giving legal advice.

"HEY!" Marco protested as seeds rained over his head. "Watch what you're doing!"

Madison kept pouring the seeds as she looked at the papers.

Polo reached out and dragged Marco out of the way. "Shh, Marco," Polo said. "She's concentrating."

"I think those are the papers that Bob gave her," Butterbean said. "Her aunt is supposed to sign them. But I don't think she has an aunt."

"Of course she has an aunt," Oscar said. "People have seen her. She can't just make up an aunt."

"Maybe," Butterbean said. "But I don't think she has an aunt here. I think her aunt is gone."

"Quiet, Butterbean," Walt said. "Her living arrangements are not our business."

"I don't know—it doesn't seem right," Polo said as Madison absentmindedly replaced the lid on their cage. It wasn't on straight, though, and there was an inch gap over the water bottle.

"See now, we could totally get out of that," Marco said. "It's practically screaming escape route."

"We can get out anyway," Polo pointed out.

"Well, yeah, but she doesn't know that," Marco said.

"Right?" Madison said to Butterbean, startling Marco and Polo into silence. "I mean, it's not a big deal. She'd sign it if she was here. So it's not like I'm doing anything wrong, right?"

"Of course not," Butterbean woofed quietly. Butterbean didn't have any problems dishing out legal advice.

Madison gave a half smile. "Look at me, talking to a dog." She clipped the leash onto Butterbean's collar. "I should just do it. It's no big deal. Right?"

"Right," Butterbean woofed again.

"I'm doing it." Madison dropped the leash and dug a pen out of her book bag. She did a few test runs on the back of her notebook, spread the papers out on the table, took a deep breath, and signed.

"Ruby S. Park. There. It's done." She gathered up the papers and shook them at Butterbean. "And if I get into trouble, I'll tell them you told me to do it."

"Wait, what?" Butterbean looked alarmed.

"Don't worry, Bean," Walt said with a smirk. "We'll come visit you in prison."

"Wait, WHAT?" Butterbean yelped.

"Don't listen to her," Oscar said. "Just go for your walk."

"Focus on the heist," Walt said.

"Right. Heist." Butterbean shot a nervous look

back over her shoulder as Madison dragged her into the hallway and closed the door.

"That was not nice," Oscar said quietly.

Walt shook her head. "That girl is going to ruin everything, isn't she?"

Oscar laughed a short, harsh laugh. "Which one, Madison or Butterbean?"

ᛣᛣᛣᛣᛣᛣᛣᛣᛣᛣᛣᛣ ᛣᛣᛣᛣᛣᛣᛣᛣ

"It's not even lying, right? Just fudging a little." Madison kept talking at the elevator. Butterbean was starting to think that she wasn't really talking to her. "It's not like I have a choice."

Butterbean nodded absently. Walt was right. She needed to focus on the heist, not on whatever Madison was doing. (Which, from what Butterbean could tell, was totally lying and not just fudging.)

"It'll be fine," Madison muttered. Butterbean stared at the floor and tried not to comment. She needed to focus on what was important. There was that weird new stain on the carpet. Butterbean sniffed it and then snorted. Biscuit. She should totally pee on it.

"I pretty much had to sign, right?" Madison said, tugging on Butterbean's leash. "If I didn't, they'd go looking for Ruby, and if that happened, it'd all be over anyway. So I might as well, right?"

Butterbean wagged her tail in what she thought was an encouraging way. If she peed on the stain, it would just take up extra time they didn't have. And they couldn't delay the heist. So she would focus. She deliberately turned her face away from the stain. Focus.

The elevator light went off and the doors opened. And Madison and Butterbean both took an involuntary step back.

Because standing in the elevator was the Coin Man.

"Ah. We meet again," he said. Madison squared her shoulders and walked into the elevator, punching the lobby button and leaning against the far wall.

"So silent," the Coin Man said, staring at her.

Madison flashed him a tight smile and turned to look straight ahead.

"Not lurking around my door today?" the Coin Man said. "Why were you doing that, I wonder?"

He turned sideways in the elevator to watch her as the doors closed. Madison kept her eyes on the lighted elevator numbers.

"I asked why you were doing that," the man said, his voice harder.

"I told you. The dog got loose. Sorry about that." Madison didn't take her eyes off the numbers.

"Ah yes. The dog. Strange that a little dog finds its way to the top floor? Almost . . . unbelievable."

Madison pressed her lips into a thin line but didn't say anything. Butterbean leaned heavily against Madison's legs. The thing was, it did sound like a ridiculous story. Too bad for Madison it was true.

"Your sweater is so sparkly," the man said, reaching out as if he was going to touch one of the buttons on Madison's cardigan.

She shrunk back closer to the wall.

"That's what you like? Sparkly things?" the man hadn't moved, but the elevator suddenly seemed a lot smaller.

"Lobby," the elevator voice said.

"See ya, bye!" Madison blurted as she squeezed out

of the opening elevator doors, almost tripping over Butterbean in her rush.

The man didn't move. He just laughed quietly as he watched her go. Then he held out his arm to stop the closing doors and strolled into the lobby.

Bob was leaning on a mop, talking to Mr. Doorman, when Madison rushed over to him.

She thrust the papers into Bob's hands, pointing at the bottom of the page. "Here you go, my aunt signed the papers, it should be all set. Okay?"

Bob stared at her. "Um, sure, but . . ."

"Great, thanks!" Madison bent down and picked Butterbean up, pushing past Mr. Doorman into the outer lobby.

Butterbean bounced along in Madison's arms as she hurried to the front door. It was different, being carried. It should have felt more relaxing, but Madison's panic was contagious.

They were almost outside when Bob's voice drifted over from the elevator area. "Oh, that? That's Ruby Park's niece. You know, on eight?"

Madison and Butterbean whirled around just in time to see Bob chatting with the Coin Man.

The man was watching them over Bob's head. A cold smile spread across his face.

"Oh great, that's just what I need," Madison said

under her breath, plopping Butterbean down onto the pavement unceremoniously. "Let's go, dog. NOW."

Butterbean didn't need to be told twice. Because now she knew two things the others didn't know. One, the Coin Man was onto them somehow. Or onto Madison at least. And two, he was leaving the building.

This was going to be the quickest walk in the history of walks.

It was heisting time.

– 13 –

"WHOOHOO HEIST DAY!" MARCO CHEERED
when Butterbean got back. "Did you see the Coin
Man? Is it go time?"

Marco was ready for some heisting. He bounced
up and down in his aquarium and didn't even care if
Madison could hear him. It was pretty obvious she
didn't speak Rat.

Butterbean nodded as Madison took the leash off.
"He just left. But UGH." She shook violently, spattering Madison with spit. "So creepy."

Madison jerked back. "Okay, I'll see you guys
soon." She suddenly looked uncomfortable. "Um.
Hopefully."

"She gave Bob the papers," Butterbean said in a low voice. "The papers that she FORGED."

"We'd better move, then. Good thing we know the Coin Man left," Oscar squawked. If the others were going to talk openly, he might as well too.

"We don't know the status of the other man," Walt said. "But Chad said that he could handle his part even if one of them was there. And he's ready. So now we just wait for Madison to leave."

The animals all turned to look at Madison, who was gathering up her book bag. She slowly looked up, as if she could feel their eyes on her. Then she set the book bag down again and stared back at them. "What?"

Nobody moved. They just blinked at her. (Except for Butterbean. She couldn't help doing a little tail wagging, too.)

"Um," Madison said. "Did I forget something?"

"We should warn her to watch out for the Coin Man," Polo said.

"She won't understand us," Walt said. "Besides, doesn't she know?"

"Watch out for the Coin Man!" Butterbean barked.

Madison picked her book bag back up. "Look, I can't stay, guys. Is that it? I'll be back. No matter what, I'll come back right after school, okay?"

"I don't think she understood you," Polo said to Butterbean.

"She's not the best listener," Butterbean said.

"No, but if she's coming back after school, we need to get moving. So she needs to go!" Walt stalked over to Madison, coiling herself around her legs and pushing her in the direction of the door. Once she saw what Walt was doing, Butterbean raced over and pushed too, in a slightly less subtle way.

"Okay, I get the hint, guys." Madison hesitated just inside the door and grinned. "You're all weirdos, you know that?"

Walt waited until the door closed and then stood stock-still, listening until she heard the elevator ding. Then she relaxed. "She's gone."

"Weirdos and CRIMINALS, am I right?" Marco said, high-fiving Polo.

Walt rolled her eyes. "Right. Everyone know what to do? Butterbean?"

Butterbean picked up her squeaky carrot and nodded. She was on hallway duty. Obviously. She was pretty clearly the queen of the hallways.

"Oscar?"

"Window," Oscar said. He snapped his beak

nervously. He wasn't big on flying outdoors, but it had to be done. He was going to be independently wealthy if it killed him.

"Marco? Polo?" Walt said.

"VENTS!" Marco and Polo cheered as they crawled out of their aquarium and raced to the sofa. "Vents, here we come. See you guys soon!"

They disappeared into the vent shaft, still cheering as they went.

"Ready, Oscar?" Walt turned her back on the vent.

"Ready," Oscar said, taking a deep breath. Walt hurried to the ledge by the dining room table and pushed at the window crank until the window opened. "Chad will open the one upstairs. Ready, Butterbean?"

Butterbean squeaked her squeaky carrot. She just wished she had a bigger part.

Walt hurried back to the front door. "Then let's go. It's on."

Marco and Polo peered through the grate into the Coin Man's apartment. The Coin Man's Number Two Guy was there, lying on the couch with his feet up on the cushions. He was looking at his phone.

"Yuck. Unsanitary," Polo said, looking at his dirty shoes on the beige sofa.

"Shoot! I was hoping he would be gone too," Marco said under his breath.

"Let's hope Chad can handle him," Polo said. She scanned the room. "He should be here any minute, right?"

"Right," Marco said. "There! Hi, Chad!" Marco waved through the grate. Chad had just emerged from the drain in the kitchen sink and was pulling himself up onto the kitchen counter. He waved a tentacle in the direction of the grate.

The man on the sofa didn't notice.

"Shh! Marco! We're heisting here!" Polo said, pulling his arm down.

"Sorry," Marco said. "SORRY, CHAD!" he yelled.

"Marco!" Polo said. "Shh. Just watch now."

She pointed at Chad, who was making his way across the counter toward the dining room. He slid off the edge of the counter, down the cabinets, and crawled across the floor. Then he pulled himself up the curtains, stretched out one long tentacle, and quietly cranked open the window.

"He's very good," Polo whispered.

Marco nodded. "Professional."

Chad slid back down the curtains onto the floor. He had just started the trek toward the kitchen when the man on the sofa put his phone aside, stretched, and stood up.

"Chad!" Polo squeaked. "Watch out!"

Chad froze, instantly changing color to match the darkness of the curtains. One minute there was a big obvious octopus lying on the carpet, and the next, he was just a dark fold in the fabric of the curtains.

"Whoa. How did he do that?" Marco breathed. "You can hardly see him." If he hadn't been watching, he never would've known Chad was there.

"Do you think he does that a lot?" Polo asked. Seeing an almost invisible Chad lying in wait made her more than a little uncomfortable.

"Shh. He's moving." Marco grabbed Polo by the arm.

The Number Two Man walked into the dining room and got an apple out of the bowl on the table. He looked at it for a second and then dropped it in disgust. He was less than a foot from Chad the whole time, but he never even looked down.

"He's going to notice the window!" Polo squealed.

"Forget the window—Oscar will be here any second," Marco said, clutching Polo by the shoulder. "He'll see Oscar! It'll blow the whole heist!"

"Chad! Do something!" Polo squeaked.

A long dark tentacle snaked out from the curtains where Chad was hidden. It snagged the end of Number Two's shoelace and pulled carefully, untying it.

The man didn't notice.

Chad's tentacle tapped Number Two on the leg, retreating back into the folds of the curtains so quickly that Marco wasn't even sure he'd seen it happen.

The man looked down and rubbed his ankle just as Oscar appeared in the window.

"Ack!" Oscar squawked, desperately flapping his wings to gain altitude again.

"Ack!" Marco gurgled, pointing at Oscar in the window.

"Ack," Number Two muttered, noticing his untied shoelace for the first time. He stomped back to the couch, threw himself down, and started tying his shoe just as Oscar made a clumsy landing and ducked behind the curtains.

Polo let out a huge sigh of relief. "This is way too stressful. We should've gotten rid of this guy too."

"No kidding," Marco said. His heart was racing, and all he was doing was standing in a vent.

The elevator in the hallway dinged.

Marco and Polo looked at each other. It was time. They were all in place.

"Ready?" Marco held up his hand.

"Ready," Polo said, high-fiving Marco.

Marco leaned out of the grate, put two fingers in his mouth, and let out a loud whistle.

"Ninth floor," the elevator woman said as the doors opened.

Butterbean and Walt cautiously peered out into the hallway.

It was empty.

Butterbean dropped her squeaky carrot in front of the elevator-door sensor, gave it an affectionate pat, and stepped over it into the hallway. She'd always liked that carrot, and now it was going to make sure they had a clean getaway.

Walt was already by the apartment door. (She was less sentimental about the carrot.) "Everyone should be in place," Walt said. "Now we just wait for the signal."

"Okay," Butterbean said. She listened as hard as she could.

From inside the apartment, they heard a thin, shrill whistle.

Butterbean and Walt looked at each other and nodded. And then they opened their mouths and started to scream.

Walt's screech sounded like she'd gotten her tail caught in the elevator door. Butterbean decided to alternate between howling and rapid-fire barking that lifted her off her feet. But the noise was incredible. The hallway had great acoustics.

They'd only been at it a minute when the door to the apartment jerked open, and the Number Two Man inside stared at them in surprise.

"Get ready," Walt yowled.

Butterbean braced herself. This was the part of the plan where the man ran out of the apartment and tried to grab them. She'd even come up with some fancy evasive maneuvers. Bouncing off the walls—that type of thing.

But there was one problem. The man didn't move.

He just stood in the doorway and stared at them like they were animal carolers with too much holiday spirit (and a defective calendar).

Butterbean frowned. "Now what?" she howled at Walt.

Walt shot a sidelong glance at Butterbean. "Me, head. You, feet."

Butterbean nodded and threw herself at the man's feet, grabbing at his pants leg and tugging him into the hallway. Walt waited until he started staggering forward, then launched herself at his face, grabbing on to his ears with both paws and twisting around his head.

"AAHHHHH!" the man screamed.

"This should do it," Walt screeched, nipping the fleshy part of his ear. She made a face. It wasn't clean.

Butterbean barked in approval and grabbed at his shoes. They weren't clean either, but a little dirt never bothered Butterbean.

When he heard the commotion in the hallway, Oscar sprang into action, pushing the curtains aside and hopping onto the table.

He scanned the room, but he didn't see Chad. That wasn't good. Chad was his contact. Without the octopus, the whole plan would fall apart.

"Curtains! Look on the floor by the curtains!"

Oscar peered up at the grate. A tiny rat arm was waving at him, and he could see a sparkly flash. Polo. Oscar looked down just in time to see part of the curtains detach and move away toward the living room. It changed color as it walked, slowly turning from a muddy-brown piece of curtain to a lighter grayish-beige octopus. Chad.

Oscar flexed his wings. He hoped he was up to this. After all, he did have a bad back.

Chad quickly pulled himself across the living room, ignoring the commotion in the hallway. Oscar decided to ignore it too. He didn't even want to know what Butterbean and Walt were doing out there.

Chad whipped a tentacle around the handle of the cabinet end table and jerked it open. The small duffel bag was there, just as Marco and Polo had said it would be. Oscar caught his breath. The treasure was real.

Chad dragged the duffel bag out, and Oscar tugged at the zipper. Gold coins spilled onto the floor.

"Nice haul," Chad said.

Oscar nodded, picking up the loose coins with his beak and dropping them back into the bag. They couldn't get sloppy. If this went well, the men wouldn't even know they'd been robbed until the animals were long gone. They couldn't leave a single trace of evidence behind.

Oscar zipped the bag back up and grabbed the handles with his feet. Then he braced himself. This was it.

He took a deep breath, flapped his wings, and lifted up into the air. Then, using every bit of strength he had, he flew slowly over to the window. Going slow wasn't part of the plan, but Oscar couldn't go any faster. He wasn't even sure he'd make it to the window in time. The bag was much heavier than the handbag he'd been practicing with.

But just when Oscar thought he'd have to give up, he made it to the window. With one last burst of strength, he flew outside, looked down, and plummeted out of sight.

₭₭ᵏₖᵏ₭ₖ ₮₭₮₭ᵏₖ₭ₖ ₭ₖᵏₖᵏₖ ₮₭₮₭

Marco and Polo watched Oscar drop like a stone. "Was it supposed to go like that?" Marco whispered.

Polo stared at the empty window. She wasn't sure. It sure didn't look like part of the plan, but she didn't want to be negative. "I think so. Looked good to me."

"Okay, if you say so," Marco said. "Give the signal."

Polo nodded and leaned as far out of the grate as she could. She put two fingers into her mouth and gave a long, low whistle.

Butterbean had a mouthful of sock when she heard the whistle from the living room. She immediately spit it out and backed away. Socks were not her chew toy of choice.

Walt leaped off the man's head and landed on the floor next to Butterbean, her legs already moving. "To the elevator! Run!"

Butterbean wheeled around and took off for the elevator, sideswiping the man and making him stumble into the wall.

Walt grabbed the squeaky carrot as Butterbean raced through the elevator door, just barely getting her tail inside before it closed.

Panting, they collapsed in a heap in the corner.

"We did it," Walt said.

Butterbean gave the carrot a weak squeak.

"Eighth floor," the elevator woman said.

"Done!" Polo said as the barking and screeching in the hallway stopped abruptly. If she craned her neck, she could see the man staggering around. She wasn't sure what Butterbean and Walt's distraction had been, but it looked effective. She turned to Marco. "Pull me back." She didn't feel comfortable leaning that far out of the grate. She didn't think she was small enough to slip through, but she was probably big enough to get stuck. And they needed to get out of there.

Marco grabbed hold of Polo's tail and pulled her back into the vent, catching her button necklace on the metalwork as he pulled. The red thread snapped, and the sparkly button fell into the room below.

"Nooo! My button!" Polo said, clutching at it as it fell. But it was no use.

Marco and Polo pressed their faces against the grate and scanned the room. "Where did it go?" Polo wailed.

"There!" Marco said, pointing. The button had bounced and was lying in the middle of the living room, next to the sofa.

"We have to get it!" Polo squealed.

Marco waved his arm desperately. "Chad!"

"Chad! The button! Get the button!" Polo shrieked.

Chad was making his way back toward the sink. He shot a look back at the grate, but he didn't stop. Now that the commotion in the hallway had ended, he didn't have much time. "I've got my butt moving," Chad said grouchily. "I can't move any faster. I'm getting rug burn as it is."

"No, not your butt! The BUTTON," Marco yelled.

Chad pulled himself onto the sink and shot the rats a nasty look before he disappeared down the drain. He didn't appreciate the comments. It wasn't like octopuses really even had butts.

"What do we do?" Polo said, staring at the sparkle on the carpet.

"We'll get you another one," Marco said, patting her on the arm. "I'll chew one off of Madison's sweater when she comes by this afternoon. You can distract her for me."

Polo shook her head. "No, it's not that. We're not supposed to leave anything behind, remember? What if the man sees it?"

Marco looked at the button uncertainly. It was very sparkly. Someone would definitely notice it.

The Number Two Man lurched back into the apartment from the hallway. His hair was standing on end like things were nesting in it, and the bottoms of his pants legs looked shredded. Whatever Walt and Butterbean had done, it was bad. He closed the door firmly behind him and flopped onto the sofa, his foot inches from the button.

It was too late.

Marco looked at Polo and then gave an awkward laugh. "It's fine. That tiny thing? They'll never notice."

But he could see the sparkle out of the corner of his eye as they turned and hurried away down the vents.

— 14 —

Butterbean was following Walt back into their apartment when Walt stopped short in the doorway. Butterbean slammed into her from behind, stumbling and falling forward onto her face.

"Hey!" Butterbean started to object, but then she caught sight of what Walt was staring at. Her jaw dropped.

The small duffel bag was on the dining room table next to the aquarium. It had been unzipped and was overflowing with coins, primarily because Oscar was inside, squawking happily and flinging gold coins in the air. It was a very undignified display.

"Oscar?" Walt said uncertainly. She'd never seen Oscar so enthusiastic before.

"Look, Walt! Gold! We're rich! I did it! And I didn't even hurt my back," Oscar crowed, flinging another coin into the air. It bonked him on the head as it fell, but he hardly flinched. He giggled in a very un-Oscar-like way.

Walt and Butterbean exchanged a concerned look. Oscar had obviously lost it.

"What's up, Oscar?" Walt said, carefully edging into the room.

Oscar hunkered deeper into the coin bag. "That rich duck on the Television does this a lot, and I always thought it looked fun!"

"Is it?" Butterbean asked, eyeing the bag. She didn't think she would be able to fit inside, but it was worth a try. She might be able to if she squeezed.

"Well, yes and no," Oscar sighed, climbing out of the bag and rearranging his ruffled wing feathers. With his feathers in place, he seemed much more like the old Oscar. "It's a very unique experience. But it does hurt when the coins hit you."

Walt jumped onto the table and nosed the bag. "It is a lot of money," she said. She dipped a paw into the bag and raked her claws through the coins. "It should be more than enough."

"Oh definitely," Oscar said. "We're independently wealthy now, no question about that." He preened and flapped his wings happily. "Our worries are over."

Butterbean stood up on her hind legs to sniff the bag. "It worked just like we planned. Those coin men won't know what hit them! Oh boy, they're going to be mad." Butterbean inspected the bag carefully. Up close, it looked like it would be too small for her. Maybe if she asked nicely, Oscar would tip the coins onto the floor so she could roll in them. It did look like a lot of fun, and Oscar seemed to be in a mood to say yes.

Butterbean cleared her throat. "Um, Oscar . . ."

"GUYS! We're back!" The rats' voices came echoing through the vents. "Did we get it? Did Oscar die?" Marco and Polo shot out of the space behind the couch and skidded to a stop at the sight of the duffel bag.

"OSCAR! WHOOHOO YOU DID IT!" Marco cheered, attempting to climb up and fist-bump Oscar.

"We weren't sure, when you fell out of sight like that," Polo said. "You dropped like a stone."

"Um. Yes," Oscar said.

"Dropped is right. Did you mean to do that?" Marco asked.

Oscar cleared his throat. "Of course I did. Time was of the essence, so I decided to go with speed, not elegance."

"Well good, we were worried!" Polo said, hugging one of Oscar's skinny legs.

Oscar patted her awkwardly on the head and averted his eyes. He hadn't actually been going for speed or elegance—he'd just been trying to stay in the air. Once he'd started falling, he'd picked up speed so quickly, he'd been afraid he wouldn't be able to stop in time. If he hadn't managed to snag the bag handle on Mrs. Food's window crank, he might have ended up a grease stain on the pavement below. A very rich grease stain, but still a grease stain.

"Thank you, Polo." Oscar cleared his throat. "So first things first. We should probably count the coins to see how many we have. Walt, you have online contacts who can help us with the next step?"

"I do."

"We'll need you to get in touch with them. See what we have to do to get the ball rolling. We don't have much time."

"We'll need to give Chad his sardines, too. We can't forget that," Polo said. She had a bad feeling that Chad was upset with them, but she wasn't sure why.

"And Wallace! We need to give him some seeds," Marco added.

"Right." Oscar nodded. "I'm so proud of you all! Our plan went off without a hitch!"

"Well, not quite," Polo said, shifting awkwardly from one foot to the other. "Not quite without a hitch."

"What? What do you mean?" Oscar clicked his beak. He was pretty sure the plan had gone perfectly.

"There was a hitch," Marco said. He thought it was pretty obvious from what Polo had said.

"My button," Polo said, putting a hand up to her neck. "The hitch is my button. The string broke, and it fell out of the grate into the living room."

"It's in the middle of the floor now," Marco said.

Oscar laughed with relief. He'd been afraid they

were going to tell him something bad. Something that would mess up the plan. "Oh, well, a button. That's a very small thing."

"But it was distinctive," Polo said. "If they find it, they'll know it was me."

"Don't be silly," Walt said.

"Polo, you're not being reasonable," Oscar said. "Even if they find it, they never saw your button! They won't have any idea it was you."

"Right." Butterbean nodded encouragingly. "They'll think it was Madison."

Four heads turned toward Butterbean.

Oscar frowned. "What do you mean, they'll think it was Madison?"

Butterbean shifted uncomfortably. She didn't like being put on the spot that way. "They'll think it was Madison, because the Coin Man knows it's her button."

Walt stalked over to Butterbean and sat down. "Explain."

Butterbean sighed. "When we were in the elevator, the Coin Man noticed her sparkly buttons. He talked about them. As soon as he sees it, he'll know it's hers."

Polo sat down hard on her haunches. She'd been afraid the Coin Man would come after her. But the idea that the Coin Man would come after Madison?

And that it was her fault? That was even worse.

"Are you sure?" Polo squeaked.

"Of course not," Oscar said. "That's ridiculous. The Coin Man didn't notice Madison's buttons."

"He totally noticed her buttons," Butterbean said.

"Oh no," Polo said weakly.

"But that's good for you, Polo," Butterbean said encouragingly. "He'll never suspect you."

"What have we done?" Polo said softly. "We have to fix this!"

"It's too late, Polo," Marco said, patting her on the shoulder. "There was no way to get it back. Madison will probably be fine."

"Marco's right, Polo," Oscar said brusquely. "It's too bad that the button was left behind. It really is. But it can't be helped. We need to move ahead with our plans."

Walt nodded. "Remember what Bob said. We don't want to go to the shelter."

"But . . ."

"I'm sure nothing will happen to her. After all, she didn't take the coins. They won't be able to blame her," Walt said.

"She'll have an alibi," Oscar said.

"I guess you're right," Polo said. "I don't feel right about it, though."

"She'll be fine," Walt said. "You'll see. She'll be here after school—you can see for yourself then."

"Oh! Right! I forgot about that," Polo said, brightening.

"In the meantime, we need to get these coins out of sight. Butterbean, do you think you can carry them into the office? I'd fly them, but . . . you know. My back," Oscar said. His back felt fine, but he was done carrying that heavy bag. He was pretty sure it made him look ridiculous.

"Sure," Butterbean said, grabbing the handle of the bag and pulling it onto the floor. Half of the coins fell out, but Butterbean didn't worry about that as she dragged the bag toward the office.

"We'll just gather those up too," Walt said, batting a gold coin in the direction of the office.

It took much longer to stash the coins away than they'd thought, and when they were through, Polo flopped down on the floor exhausted. "Wake me up when Madison gets here," she said, closing her eyes.

Marco looked at the clock on the wall and frowned. "Okay, but . . ." he said, looking worried. "Isn't she supposed to be back now?"

They all turned and looked at the clock and then at the door. There was no sound from the hallway outside.

Polo looked back at the clock. "Walt?"

Walt's eyes were still on the door. "She's late. It's not a problem."

"The clock says she should be here," Polo said.

"My bladder says she should be here," Butterbean said.

"She's probably fine," Marco said weakly. "Maybe they made her stay late?"

"They didn't make her stay late," Polo said, standing up. "Something is wrong. I'm going to find out what's happened."

Polo turned and marched toward the vent without another word.

"I'm going too," Marco said, hurrying after her.

"I think you're overreacting, Polo," Walt said.

"Well, we'll see," Polo said as she climbed into the vent. Marco scurried after her with one last apologetic look at Walt.

"She's probably fine," Oscar said, looking out of the window at the street below. He saw lots of adult people, but no small, child-sized people. "It was just a button. Who would even notice that?"

"The Coin Man," Butterbean said, her head on her paws. She was stationed by the front door, nose pressed to the gap underneath. "The Coin Man will notice."

"Well, it doesn't matter. She wasn't part of our plan anyway," Oscar said. "Not to be mean, but we need to look out for ourselves. We don't have Mrs. Food to take care of us anymore."

"If something happens to Madison, we don't have anybody to take care of us anymore," Butterbean grumbled. She really needed to pee.

Oscar looked back out of the window. There was no doubt now that something was very wrong. Madison had never been this late.

"Ahem, excuse me?" A small voice came from the direction of the vent. "Knock knock?"

"Who's there!" Butterbean said, whirling around. A small rat was standing nervously by the couch. And even though he'd said "knock knock," it didn't sound like he was telling a joke.

"Um, I'm Wallace. I'm here about Marco and Polo?" Wallace cleared his throat. "I met them in the vents?"

Walt jumped down from the top of the couch and landed next to Wallace, who was visibly startled. "You know Marco and Polo?"

"Um, yes?" Wallace eyed the vent like he was planning to make a dash for it.

"They're not here, unfortunately. Would you like

to wait?" Walt leaned away from the rat. She was trying to be as nonthreatening as possible. Wallace didn't seem like a rat who'd had a lot of experience with cats. Or at least not good experiences.

Wallace cleared his throat and clutched his hands in front of his chest. "Yes, I realize that. That's why I came. There seems to be some sort of . . . incident going on? In the apartment on the top floor? I thought you might like to know."

"What's happening?" Oscar flew over and landed on Wallace's other side. He loomed over the rat, eyeing him carefully. He wasn't worried about being non-threatening.

Wallace swallowed. "I'm not sure. I don't go to those vents. But I saw Marco and Polo go up there, and . . . well, there's a lot of noise. Bad sounds. I'm not sure."

Butterbean pawed at the front door. "Walt! Open! We need to go now!"

"Butterbean, wait." Oscar turned to Walt. "Maybe Chad can help?"

"I don't know—Butterbean might be right," Walt said, looking at Wallace. If he had risked coming to a cat's apartment, the situation must be bad.

"Maybe we should—" Walt started, but she was cut off by a screeching noise in the vent.

A screeching noise that was coming from Marco.

He skidded into the room and grabbed Walt's leg, clutching at it in desperation.

"WALT!" he screamed. "It's Polo! We went to Madison's apartment to check on her, but she wasn't there! But there were signs something bad had happened, so we decided to check on the Coin Man, and he got her! He found the button! And it's bad! Oh, Walt!" Marco sobbed.

Walt put her paws on either side of Marco's shoulders. "Marco. Calm down. Where's Polo?"

Marco shook uncontrollably. "Oh, Walt. Polo's dead!"

BUTTERBEAN GAVE A LOW MOAN. OSCAR PUT HIS wing around Marco and led him over to Butterbean's squeaky carrot. "Sit down, Marco. Now, you're sure she's dead?"

"The Coin Man got her! Of course she's dead!" Marco wailed. He sat down on the squeaky carrot, which emitted a long, plaintive squeal. "She must be."

Oscar and Walt exchanged hopeful glances.

"So she could still be alive?" Walt asked. "There's a chance?"

Marco sniffled and wiped his nose on the squeaky carrot stem. "Hardly any chance. You weren't there, Walt. It was bad."

Walt's whiskers trembled. "Okay, but hardly any is still a chance. Even if it was bad, it might not have been *dead* bad."

"The Coin Man kicked at her. She went flying across the room." Marco's eyes welled up. "Do you think she could've survived that? He was going after her when I left."

Walt winced. That didn't sound good at all. But she wasn't about to tell Marco that. "Marco, we don't know what happened next. Polo is a very resilient young rat. We can't give up on her yet."

"Walt is right," Oscar said. "We have to do something." He looked at the window thoughtfully. "The window in the Coin Man's apartment may not be open anymore. And even if it is, it would be too easy for me to be seen." He looked at Wallace, who was eyeing the vent like he wanted to leave. "Wallace, can you take me to the Coin Man's apartment?"

Marco blinked. "What? You just said the window might be closed. How are you going to get in?"

"Through the vent, of course," Oscar said, fluffing his feathers. "I should fit. You both did it. It will be fine."

"You're going in the vent? YOU?" Marco said. "You don't even like to have your cage door closed."

"Well, it can't be helped," Oscar said. "It's the only way. If we can rescue Polo, it's worth it."

Wallace looked from Oscar to Marco uncertainly. "I can show you how to get there," Wallace said. "If you really want to go."

"I'll do it!" Marco said, standing up and wiping his eyes. "You don't need Wallace to show you. I'm not afraid to go back. I owe it to Polo."

Wallace shrugged. "I'll go too, if it's all the same to you. Just to make sure you don't get turned around wrong." He didn't like the idea of Marco and a bird blundering around in his vents unaccompanied. It sounded like a recipe for disaster.

"Thank you, Wallace." Oscar put one foot into the vent and tried not to think about how much he hated vents. Or how narrow they were. Or how dusty they were. And he definitely couldn't think about how likely he was to get trapped inside them forever. When he was a fledgling, he'd heard stories about an aunt who'd gotten stuck in a chimney once. He'd had nightmares about it more than a few times. But he had to think of Polo now. If she was still alive, they had to do something.

"Yeah, um, excuse me," Marco muttered, finally pushing Oscar aside. He took a few steps into the vent then looked back. "Oscar? You coming?"

Oscar took a deep breath and climbed in. It wasn't that bad, actually, especially knowing the exit was right behind him.

"I'm going too," Walt said, slinking over and wriggling inside. "Move over, Oscar." It was going to be a tight fit, but nothing she hadn't done before. She'd once managed to fit herself into a tissue box. One of the pop-up ones, not one of the more spacious horizontal kind.

Oscar squawked in dismay. He wished he'd brought a paper bag to breathe into.

"I'm going too," Butterbean said, hurrying over to the opening. She wasn't about to be left behind.

Butterbean managed to squeeze into the vent up to her ears, but getting her whole head inside was trickier than she'd thought. That didn't mean she couldn't do it. It was just a matter of willpower.

"Bean, no," Walt said, her eyes gleaming in the darkness. "You need to stay here. We need someone to guard the apartment."

"No, I'm going too," Butterbean said, twisting her neck to try to get her whole head inside the vent. "I know I can squish. I've got a squishy head. Just give me a second."

"But what if Bob comes back?" Walt said. The last thing they needed was for Butterbean to get stuck in the vent. "You've got a powerful bark. We need you here, to bark for us if there's trouble."

Butterbean stopped and pulled her head back out

of the vent. She hated to admit it, but it was probably for the best. Her head wasn't even the widest part of her body. "Fine," she finally said, staring at the floor. "I'll stay here. I'll be ready to bark."

"Good. Thank you, Butterbean," Walt said. "You guard the coins." Walt waited a minute to make sure Butterbean was really staying behind and then turned and disappeared down the vent.

Butterbean suddenly sat up straight. The coins. Her eyes gleamed. She knew just what to do. "Right, I'll guard the coins!"

Polo sat in the dark thinking about her life choices. Ever since Mrs. Food had gone away, things seemed to have taken a bad turn. And Polo was pretty sure a lot of it had to do with some questionable choices on her part.

Madison, for instance. It had seemed like a very good idea to go check on her when she didn't show up. And when Polo had seen the trashed apartment and realized Madison was gone, it had seemed like a very good idea to go check the Coin Man's apartment.

And when she realized he'd kidnapped Madison, it had seemed like a very good idea to throw herself repeatedly against the vent grate until she broke through and fell kamikaze-style into the living room. And since she was down there anyway, within striking distance of the Coin Man's ankles, attacking those ankles had seemed like the logical thing to do. Anybody would have done the same thing, right? It had all seemed like a very good idea—until he'd kicked her across the room, that is.

The last thing she remembered was hearing Marco screaming as she flew through the air. She'd thought it would be the last thing she ever heard. But instead she'd woken up in Madison's pocket, so in a way she'd been pretty lucky.

Polo sighed. If her bad choices had gotten her into this mess, she was just going to have to make some good choices to get out of it. She stuck her nose out of the pocket and looked around. It was dark, and Madison seemed to be sitting on the bathroom floor. Interesting choice. Maybe Madison should evaluate her life choices too. Polo shook her head. That wasn't fair. Madison wouldn't even be in this situation if it wasn't for Polo and her button.

"You okay, little guy?" Madison said in a low voice. "You awake?"

Polo craned her neck to look up at Madison. Her face was streaky looking, like she'd been crying. Polo twitched her whiskers at her.

"I thought I'd better get you out of the way before he kicked you again." Madison gave her a weak smile. "Now you're stuck with me, but it's better than being stomped."

Polo couldn't argue with that.

"You know, you look like another rat I know. Down on the fourth floor. I'm supposed to be taking care of her right now." She sniffled. "Two rats, actually, and a bunch of other animals."

"It's me. And don't worry—Marco will find us," Polo squeaked softly. She wasn't sure it was true, though. Marco hadn't been screaming like he was planning a rescue. He'd been screaming like he was running away and never coming back.

"They're not going to let us out, little guy," Madison said softly, tentatively touching Polo's ear. "They think I stole from them. But I didn't do it, I swear."

"I know," Polo squeaked. She crawled out of Madison's jacket pocket and climbed onto her knee. She tried to look understanding, but it wasn't easy. She mostly felt guilty. And she really wished she'd learned to speak Human. Speaking another language was always useful.

Madison sniffled again and wiped her nose. "And the worst part is, except for those animals, nobody's

even going to miss me. Not for a long time. Can I tell you a secret?"

"Sure," Polo squeaked.

"My aunt that I live with? I don't exactly live with her anymore." Madison watched Polo's reaction carefully. "Are you shocked?" Madison whispered.

Well, no. But Polo tried to look shocked. She actually wished she had someone to high-five. She KNEW there was nobody else in that apartment.

She and Butterbean had been right. She just hoped that she would be able to see Butterbean again to tell her.

"I did, but she's in the army. And she got deployed. So she set it up so I would stay with my friend Christie's family while she was gone. It was all planned out. Then right when she left, their grandma got sick, and so they couldn't take me. So I just . . . didn't tell anybody. I didn't say anything to my aunt, and I told Christie's parents that my aunt had found someone else to take me. And then I just stayed at my aunt's place. So there's not even anyone to miss me."

Polo's heart sank. As glad as she was to be right, it made everything worse. Because that meant it was all up to her. There were no parents coming to help Madison. No aunt. No one. She couldn't even depend on Marco and the others to come help her.

She and Madison were totally alone.

"I don't know why you can't just fly," Marco grumbled. Oscar was taking forever. His bird feet were not made for walking in slippery metal vents.

"I've told you, Marco, it's too low for me to fly. I'll hit my head. Or rather, hit my head AGAIN." Oscar had already given in to Marco's pestering once, and it had gone pretty much how he'd expected—with Oscar smacking his head against the top of the vent. The resulting clang had been so loud that some people in an apartment nearby heard it and peeked through the grate. They hadn't expected to see a mynah bird. (They didn't think they had, either. They'd decided Oscar was either a pigeon or a mutant cockroach. Luckily, Oscar had been out of earshot by the time they'd come to that conclusion.)

Once he'd gotten over his initial panic, Oscar had to admit the vents were a lot cleaner than he had expected, and a lot less claustrophobic. Even so, he was going to need a good bath when everything was said and done. And there was no guarantee Madison would be there to change the water in his dish. Maybe Walt knew how to work the faucets.

"It's just ahead, through that up vent," Wallace said, ignoring the squabbling. "I'm going to leave you here. Marco will be able to show you the apartment grates."

"Thank you, Wallace," Walt said as she squeezed past him to slip into the up vent. "We'll be sure to bring you extra seeds when this is all over."

"Uh, thanks." Wallace flattened himself against the wall as Walt squeezed by. He was not used to the idea of a cat in the vents, no matter how polite Walt was. It made his stomach squirm just thinking about it.

Oscar hopped up to the next floor and shuffled over to the grate as quickly as he could, with Walt right behind him. Marco was waiting, arms crossed and foot tapping impatiently.

He pointed out through the grate. "See? That's the living room," he whispered. "The Coin Man and the other guy are still there."

Oscar put an eye to the grate and peered around the room. The men were angry and arguing, but Oscar didn't pay any attention to them. Right now he was worried about one thing and one thing only. Polo.

"Madison's not there," Walt said, peering through the grate next to him.

Two things. Oscar was worried about two things. Polo and Madison.

"I'm betting she's behind that door." Walt nodded toward a door on the other side of the living room. It had a chair wedged under the handle. Oscar shivered. That did not look good.

"You know what else I don't see?" Walt continued, her voice low. "I don't see a dead rat. Or any rat, wounded or otherwise. I don't see Polo."

Oscar cleared his throat and looked over at Marco. He wasn't paying attention to them—he seemed intent on listening to the men arguing. Oscar edged closer to Walt. "They could have ... disposed of her," he said quietly. The last thing he wanted was for Marco to overhear him.

Walt shook her head. "I don't think those guys would've bothered. And look down there." She nodded toward the floor right below the grate. Oscar had to crane his neck to see what she was pointing at. It was a mousetrap.

"They wouldn't have put that there if they thought they got her."

Walt sounded confident, but Oscar wasn't so sure. He just hoped she was right.

He scuttled over to Marco, cringing with every step. Skidding on the metal floor was so undignified. "Marco. Is there another grate?"

"SHH!" Marco hissed, putting his hands over Oscar's beak. "Listen—I think this is important!"

"No excuses." The Coin Man's voice was sharp, and he was pointing aggressively at the second man. The Coin Man didn't touch him, but Number Two flinched with every jab as if he had. "One. How did she get in? Two. How did she get the coins? Three. Where are they now? And most importantly, why did you not notice? These are questions that I want answered, now."

The Coin Man crossed the living room and pulled

the chair away from the door. "If you can't answer, she will."

"Quick, to the other grate!" Marco said, hurtling himself down the vent. "We need to see!"

Marco and Walt scurried away, with Oscar awkwardly slipping along behind. He arrived just in time to see the Coin Man crouching down next to Madison. She didn't look like she'd been harmed, but she was obviously not okay. Oscar scanned the room. There was no sign of Polo.

"Little girl, you have made a very big mistake."

Madison tried not to react, but she couldn't help but flinch a little at the Coin Man's words.

"It was a funny game to you, stealing from me? It is not a game now, believe me." The man's voice was very low, and the animals had to strain to hear him. He wasn't shouting. He didn't even raise his voice. But something in the way he spoke made Oscar shiver.

"I will be back in one hour. When I return, you will tell me where the coins are. Understand? That is your only option. If you want to survive."

He stared at Madison until she nodded hesitantly.

"Good. And to be clear, I know all about you, Miss Madison Park. I know you are alone. No one will miss you. No one knows you are here. Remember that. No one is coming to save you. So you will do what I say."

Madison nodded again, biting her lip to steel herself. She refused to look away from him.

The Coin Man stood up and opened the door. "One hour," he said again, closing the door and locking it behind him.

Madison waited until she was sure he was gone and then broke out in a strangled sob. "I don't have the coins!" she whispered. "What am I going to do?"

Polo poked a head out of Madison's pocket and scrambled back up onto her knee. "We'll think of a plan," Polo said quietly. She had no idea what, but they had to try something. Anything. And they only had an hour.

"POLO!" a voice shrieked from the vent grate. "IT'S POLO! YOU'RE ALIVE!"

Polo's head jerked up, and she leaned back to look up at the grate. "Marco?" She stood on her hind legs and waved excitedly. "MARCO!" she screamed. "I'm okay! It's me!"

"What are you doing?" Madison said, staring at Polo like she'd sprouted an extra head. It was one thing to have a rat quietly comforting you. It was something entirely different when that rat started to scream and wave at someone you couldn't see.

Madison peered up at the grate.

If she squinted, she thought she could just make

out eyes staring back at her from the darkness. Three pairs of eyes.

She blinked. The eyes were still there. And was that a tiny arm waving through the grate? That didn't seem possible.

Madison scrambled to her feet and climbed up onto the sink to get a closer look, carefully putting Polo on the counter first.

"No way," Madison breathed. "No way."

Those were definitely eyes. And they were looking right back at her. If she didn't know better, she'd say they looked just like the cat and bird and rat that she'd been taking care of. But that was ridiculous.

"Do you have a plan?" Polo squeaked from her new perch on the soap dish. "We have an hour."

"Um. Maybe?" Marco didn't sound like he had a plan.

"Don't worry—we've got a rescue all planned out," Walt said. Her voice was much more reassuring. "Just wait there. We'll be back soon."

Polo cheered and did a little dance on the soap dish. Carefully, so she didn't slip. But this was the best news she'd had all day, and a small celebration was in order.

Madison watched Polo's dance number and then sat down on the cabinet with a thump. That had definitely sounded like a cat. And now the rat was dancing. She was losing it.

"We'll be back! Just hold on," Marco squeaked. "Bye!"

As Polo and Madison watched, the three faces disappeared from the grate.

Madison stared at the empty grate until a small pattering on her hand caught her attention. It was the rat, and it looked like it was patting her on the hand to console her.

"It'll be okay, Madison!" Polo squeaked.

Madison gave a small smile. Even if she was crazy, the rat looked so optimistic. She hoped it knew something she didn't.

"Okay, Walt, what's up?" Oscar said after they'd slipped back down to the eighth-floor vents. "That all sounded good, but do you really have a plan?" He tried his best not to sound disapproving, but he couldn't see how Walt could possibly have a plan. "I don't want to give Polo false hope."

Walt sat down with a sigh. "I do have a plan, and I think it could work. But you're not going to like it. You're not going to like it one bit."

Oscar puffed his feathers out indignantly. If the

plan saved Polo, how could he not like it? "Well, what is it?"

"I can only think of one thing that will work." Walt's face was grim. "We need to pull off another heist. An anti-heist. We need to give the coins back."

— 16 —

"You want to do what?" Butterbean sat up abruptly, gold coins sliding off her tummy. "Give it back? *Back* back? Are you crazy?"

They'd found Butterbean in the office, rolling in the bag of gold coins. She was obviously taking her guard duty very seriously. She hadn't let them out of her sight. Butterbean stood up, slipping on the pile as she trotted out of the office and over to Oscar. "But we can't give it back, can we, Oscar? We're independently wealthy now. We need them." She blinked with her best puppy dog eyes.

Oscar cleared his throat and looked away. "I think we have to," he said reluctantly. He couldn't believe he was saying it. The whole heist had been such a success. It was his greatest achievement. And now it was all going down the drain, just because of one little slip up.

Oscar had seen heist shows on the Television before, so he thought he'd known all the possible pitfalls. But he'd never once seen an organized crime gang have to pull an anti-heist and return the money.

But they were going to do it. It was already in the works.

Walt had run the plan by Chad, who had agreed to help out, as long as there were no more comments about his butt. Oscar wasn't sure what that was about, but he was happy to agree. He'd never even noticed Chad's butt. (Although now he felt like he needed to take a look.) Once they'd all solemnly sworn not to say a single word about his backside, Chad was in.

Now all they had to do was get Butterbean on board.

Luckily, Marco knew just what to say. He stepped forward and took Butterbean by the paw. "Butterbean, we have to do this. For Polo. And for Madison. We can't let those men win. Don't think of it as giving the coins back. This is a rescue mission."

Butterbean's ears perked up. She'd always wanted to go on a rescue mission. It was practically her dog destiny.

Butterbean licked Marco's paw in excitement (along with half of his middle section. Marco pretended not to notice).

"Why didn't you say so? Rescue mission? Sign me up!" Maybe she'd get one of those little barrels to wear around her neck—she'd seen Television dogs wearing those on lots of rescue missions. Of course it would have to be a small one, but Butterbean didn't mind.

Walt patted Butterbean on the back. "Good. Oscar, you'll need to get these coins back in the bag."

Oscar nodded and hurried back into the office.

Walt sat down. "Now, Butterbean, what we're planning is a three-pronged attack. Part one, Operation Distract. Part two, Operation Divide and Conquer. And part three, Operation Outside Authorities. Got it?"

"Got it." Butterbean hoped she would be part of Operation Distract. Distracting was her specialty. She wasn't so great at division.

"You're Operation Distract, with me," Walt said. Butterbean gave a small cheer. Walt ignored it. "Oscar, are the coins ready?"

"Done," Oscar called back from the office, one foot on the coin bag.

"Good. Chad's in place, so if you could just fly them up, we'll be set. Wallace, Marco, ready for vent duty?"

"Ready!" Marco fist-bumped Wallace (who wasn't

quite ready) and raced into the vents. He was feeling much more optimistic now that he knew that Polo was alive.

"Wait, what? Me?" Wallace looked around nervously. He hadn't realized he was part of the plan. He was thinking of himself as more of an interested bystander.

"Wallace, COME ON!" Marco yelled impatiently, his voice echoing in the vent.

"Oop. Okay. I mean . . . okay." Wallace scurried toward the vent after Marco.

"Um, Walt?" Oscar's voice came from overhead. "Potential problem here."

Oscar had the bag in his claws and was hovering in the air. He wasn't going anywhere, just hovering. "I'm having some trouble getting airborne," he said. "I can't seem to gain altitude."

Walt's eyes widened. Oscar was approximately three feet off the floor, which was not going to cut it. Not when they needed to go to an apartment on the ninth floor. "Well, you're going to need to gain five stories of altitude. Fast. Or the plan won't work."

"Yes, I do realize that," Oscar said, flapping his wings energetically. He still didn't move.

"Um, about that," he said finally. "I don't see myself gaining five stories of altitude."

"But you did it before!" Walt couldn't believe Oscar was being so difficult. What was five stories to a bird? Five stories was nothing!

Oscar gave a sad smile. "Yes, that's true. But before I was going down. Down isn't a problem. Up is." He flapped even more enthusiastically and rose another six inches off the floor.

"I volunteer!" Butterbean barked suddenly. "I'll do it! Oh, please let me. I just have to take it upstairs, right? It'll be fine! I can do it!"

Walt and Oscar both looked at Butterbean doubtfully.

"There's no rule that it has to go in the window, right? We just need to get the bag up there?"

"Oscar?" Walt said.

"I think that would be best," Oscar said, sinking to the floor. "I'll stay here and watch the surveillance cameras. You'll need to know if the Coin Man comes back."

"That's actually a better idea," Walt said grudgingly. "We do need to know that. Okay, ready, Bean?"

"YAY!" Butterbean cheered, jumping up and dragging the bag away from Oscar.

"Keep cool, Bean," Walt said, going to the door and pushing the handle down. "Let us know the minute he comes back," she called to Oscar over her shoulder.

"Will do," he said, walking slowly to the remote. He really did have a bad back.

Butterbean was already halfway down the hallway when Walt slipped out of the door. Butterbean jumped up and hit the elevator button.

"Hope it's empty!" She hopped nervously from

one foot to another while she waited. "Man, I hope the Coin Man isn't in it when it opens. That would be the worst!"

"Don't be silly," Walt said, but she felt just as anxious. So many things could go wrong. She hadn't had time to think though all the possible problems. Anything could happen.

The elevator binged, and Walt held her breath. The doors opened.

It wasn't empty. Mrs. Power Walker was there, marching in place.

Butterbean didn't hesitate. She dragged the bag into the elevator and sat down next to Mrs. Power Walker, wagging her tail and lolling her tongue out of the side of her mouth. Walt slipped in behind her.

Mrs. Power Walker looked down at Butterbean and smiled. "Oh, hello again. Eighth floor, right?" she said, pushing the button for Butterbean.

Butterbean wagged her tail harder. Eighth floor was not right, but she wasn't going to say anything. She didn't want to attract attention.

"Sixth floor," the elevator voice said.

The doors opened. Bob the maintenance guy was standing in the hallway. He looked from Mrs. Power Walker to Butterbean to the bag. Then he looked at Walt. Walt shrugged.

"I'll, uh, take the next one," Bob said awkwardly, scratching the back of his head.

"Bye!" Mrs. Power Walker said cheerily, pushing the close door button.

"Bye." Bob frowned at Butterbean and Walt. "Hey, wait a minute," he said, narrowing his eyes as the doors closed.

"Oops!" Mrs. Power Walker said to Butterbean conspiratorially. She giggled. Butterbean thumped her tail on the floor.

"Seventh floor," the elevator voice said.

"Bye, you two," Mrs. Power Walker said as she power walked out of the elevator.

Butterbean waited until the doors had closed before she jumped up and hit the button for the ninth floor. Walt rolled her eyes.

"What? I didn't want to be rude!" Butterbean said, sitting back down.

🐾 🐾 🐾 🐾 🐾 🐾 🐾 🐾 🐾 🐾

Marco and Wallace peered through the grate into the Coin Man's apartment.

Wallace looked like he might throw up. "I shouldn't even be here. I can't believe you talked me into this. I ONLY GO TO THE EIGHTH FLOOR! I TOLD YOU THAT."

"Yeah, but it's fine, see?" Marco said, patting Wallace on the shoulder. "Nothing's happening yet! It's just that guy. Number Two."

Through the grate they could see the second man perched nervously on the couch, cradling a drink in his hands. He also looked like he might throw up.

"Oh and look, it's Chad! Hi, Chad!" Marco screamed, sticking his arm through the grate and waving.

Chad pulled himself up into the sink. He put two of his tentacles to his eyes and then pointed at the grate in a classic "I'm watching you" motion.

Marco waved a little less enthusiastically. "Looking good, Chad. Thanks for doing this!"

Wallace clutched Marco's arm. "Should you be yelling and waving like that? With THAT PERSON sitting there?"

Marco didn't get a chance to answer.

The elevator dinged outside. Marco looked at Wallace. "Here we go." He put his fingers in his mouth and whistled.

Butterbean dragged the coin bag into a shadowy nook near the elevator. "Same plan as before?" She didn't really love the idea of another mouthful of dirty sock, but for

Polo? Number Two's dirty socks were no problem.

Walt grinned. "I thought we'd try something different this time." She bent down and whispered in Butterbean's ear.

Butterbean wagged her tail. She liked the new plan.

When they heard Marco's whistle, she stood on her hind legs and rang the bell.

The Number Two Man was so startled by the doorbell that his hand jerked, sloshing part of his drink down his front. Muttering to himself, he put the drink onto the coffee table and hurried to the door, wiping his hands on his pants as he went.

He opened the door cautiously and looked out into the hallway.

Marco and Wallace pressed their faces to the grate to get a clear look.

There, in the hallway, sat Walt and Butterbean. They sat perfectly still in front of the door, staring silently at the man.

He went pale. "Oh no. No," he said, backing away. Then he slammed the door in their faces.

Marco and Wallace looked at each other. "I wonder if that's what was supposed to happen?" Marco said.

"Well, shoot. That's not what was supposed to happen," Walt muttered, twitching her tail. She'd been sure that if they sat quietly, he would come out to see what was going on. But no. "How are we supposed to get him out here? Ring the bell again, Butterbean."

Butterbean stood up and rang the bell again.

No one answered.

"We should've just gone for the ankles," Butterbean said. "Or we could've knocked him down, and I could've done the nostril probe."

"Hey! Hey, Walt! It's Marco! Up here!"

Walt and Butterbean peered up at the ceiling, following the voice to the corner, where they could see Marco peeking out from a small grate.

"Boy, you freaked him out," Marco said. "Was it supposed to happen like that?"

"Obviously not," Walt said grouchily. "I didn't think he'd have such bad manners."

"Okay, well, don't worry. Chad said he has a plan," Marco explained. "When I whistle, try the doorbell thing again. Chad said he's had it with this guy, and he's not wasting any more time. He's going to take him out."

"Oookay," Walt said. That didn't sound terrific. In fact, "take him out" sounded really, really bad.

"So Chad . . . um. He's okay, right?" Marco interrupted her thoughts. "'Cause he sounded super grumpy. I mean SUPER grumpy. And maybe a little scary." More than a little, actually.

Walt hesitated. "Yeah, he's a good guy. Octopus. Good octopus," she corrected herself. But now that she thought about it, how well did she know Chad? Not that well, to be honest. And a grumpy octopus was capable of doing, well, anything.

"I guess we'll just wait for the signal, then," Walt said, trying to sound confident. The whole thing had gone completely off the rails.

She just had to hope for the best. It was up to Chad now.

– 17 –

CHAD INCHED HIS WAY THROUGH THE PIPE. He couldn't believe he had gotten mixed up in this whole mess. And for a few measly sardines! It absolutely was not worth it. Still, it would be a good story later on, as long as the others didn't get themselves killed. Actually, it would be a good story either way. But he might as well try to keep them alive. Make himself the hero. Happy endings always went over better in octopus circles.

Chad slipped up the pipe and out through the sink drain overhead. Just as he'd thought, he was in the bathroom. And judging from the terrible decor, he was still in the Coin Man's apartment.

A girl gasped. Madison, he guessed. Nice to see that she was alive, but he didn't have time to chat.

"Holy cow, what is that?" Madison squealed, staring at him. Rude. Chad ignored her and slithered up to the medicine cabinet. He didn't have a lot of time to waste. He rummaged around on the shelves, examining medicine bottles and tossing them aside.

"Oh, that's just Chad!" A voice from the floor piped up. "Hey, Chad! It's me, Polo!" Chad looked

over his shoulder and saw Polo hopping up and down and waving. He gave a polite wave with one of his unoccupied tentacles while he uncapped a medicine bottle with the others. Just what he was looking for. He broke a pill in half.

"What are you doing in here?" Polo crawled up onto the cabinet next to him. "Are you rescuing us? Can I do anything to help?"

Chad frowned and tossed the rest of the pills aside. "No, I've got what I need. Sleeping pills. I'm going to drug his drink."

Polo looked at the broken pill. "Isn't that dangerous?"

Chad snorted. "I'm not even giving him a whole pill. Just enough to knock him out while we set up the room. Sheesh." Rats could be so jittery.

"Oh, good," Polo said, trying to look relieved. "So we just wait here, then?"

Chad slid back into the sink. "Right. Stay alert. You may need to move fast."

He disappeared down the drain, and then one eye popped back up. "Polo."

"Yeah?" Polo peered down at him.

"Glad you're not dead."

Polo smiled. "Yeah, me too."

When Chad crawled back up into the kitchen sink, the man was on the couch, looking from the front door to the bathroom door, like he was watching a tennis match. He seemed nervous, to say the least.

"I don't get it," Wallace said, watching the man. "What's he so freaked out about? Walt and Butterbean aren't scary. Well, maybe Walt, but Butterbean? Her name's BUTTERBEAN, for goodness sake."

Marco shrugged. "Humans are weird."

Chad had already made his way over to the edge of the couch and was waving a tentacle at Marco in an irritated way, like he'd been doing it a long time. He was also making gestures with his other tentacles that Marco was pretty sure were bad words.

"Sorry, Chad!" Marco yelled.

He put his hands in his mouth and whistled.

The doorbell rang.

The man's hand clenched the sofa so hard his knuckles turned white. He stared at the front door like it was going to explode.

The bell rang again. And again. And again. It sounded to Marco like Butterbean was just bouncing between the floor and the doorbell over and over. She could be very enthusiastic.

Finally, the Number Two Man had had enough.

He got up, braced himself for a second, and then walked slowly toward the door.

Marco whistled again.

The man cautiously put his hand on the door handle, and then, taking a deep breath, he pulled it open. The cat and the dog sat in the doorway, just as they had before. And just as they had before, they silently stared back at him.

No one moved. No one except Chad.

In a flash, he slithered up to the coffee table and dropped the broken sleeping pill into the man's drink. Then he speed-inched his way back to the sink. Once he was safely inside, Marco whistled again.

Without a sound, and without even looking at each other, Walt and Butterbean turned in unison and walked away down the hallway.

The man stood slack-jawed, watching them go. Then he slammed the door, raking his hands through his hair. He lurched back across the room, threw himself onto the couch, grabbed his drink, and gulped it down in one swift movement.

Marco and Wallace watched from the grate.

Chad watched from the sink.

Number Two's eyelids drooped. In just a few minutes they had shut, and his head flopped back onto the sofa.

Marco whistled again as Chad scooted across the living room floor.

"Stupid carpets," he muttered as he went. "Do you realize I have rug burns on THREE of my tentacles because of this? THREE. And I hardly even KNOW you guys."

He reached up and opened the door. Walt and Butterbean rushed in, dragging the bag behind them.

"These rug burns are going to cost you EXTRA SARDINES," Chad grumbled.

"Operation Distract is complete!" Butterbean trotted to the couch and dropped the bag with a thump. "In this end table here, Chad?"

"Right." Chad unzipped the bag and then crawled onto the man's lap. He reached a tentacle down toward the bag. "Actually, scooch it over a bit first."

Butterbean nudged the bag closer to the man's foot. Chad grabbed a bunch of coins with his tentacles and stuffed them into the man's pockets. The man didn't even move.

"He's not dead, right?" Butterbean said, jumping up and examining him.

"With half a pill? Hardly. We'll be lucky if we make it out of here before he wakes up," Chad scoffed, passing coins from tentacle to tentacle. It was like he had his own relay system set up. It was very effective.

"Hey, Chad?" Walt said, peering inside the end table. "Was this stuff in here when you took the bag originally?"

"What stuff?" Chad flung the last few coins onto the man's lap like he was throwing confetti and inched his way over to the end table. He peered inside. "Oh, that stuff? Yeah, I guess. Why, did you want that, too?"

Walt shook her head. "No, we're not touching this." She turned to Butterbean. "This is bad news. We've got to get out of here."

Butterbean cocked her head. "Why, what is it?"

"Trouble," Walt said. "Big trouble."

Oscar sat on the floor in front of the Television watching the surveillance feed.

"This is fine," he said to himself. "This is fine." He didn't feel fine, though.

He knew that watching the feed was important. And he knew that criminal masterminds usually left the grunt work to their minions. But he didn't like the idea that the others were up there alone.

A figure on the Television caught his eye.

Oscar jumped up with a squawk. He'd only seen him through the grate, but he would recognize him forever.

The Coin Man was back.

Butterbean pawed at the inside of the end table. She could see what looked like winter hats, and something metallic underneath. She frowned. "Why are hats trouble?"

She pawed at the hats again. A black ski mask fell onto the floor. "Should I try it on? I'll look like a robber!" Butterbean joked, and then caught herself. "Oh. I'll look like a robber."

"Exactly." Walt didn't sound like she was joking.

Butterbean nosed the metallic things. "And these must be?"

"Guns," Walt said. "Those are guns of some sort."

"Then that means—"

"That means we need to go. Now."

"Okey dokey, then," Butterbean said, trotting over to the door.

Walt looked around for Chad, who was examining the contents of the kitchen cabinets. "Chad? Time to—"

"OUT! OUT NOW!" Oscar flew in through the window, collapsing on the couch in a dramatic crash landing that made everyone duck for cover. "The Coin Man is on his way."

"What?" Walt and Butterbean stared at Oscar in panic.

The elevator bell dinged in the hallway.

Oscar's eyes widened. "The Coin Man is here."

– 18 –

WALT LEAPED TO HER FEET. "OSCAR, GO! START Operation Outside Authorities!" she screeched. "It's all up to you now!"

"Operation Outside Authorities, check," Oscar echoed, launching himself out of the window.

Chad scooted into the kitchen sink in record time. "I'm out of here. Good luck," he called, sliding into the drain. "You'll need it."

Butterbean turned to Walt. "What about us?"

Walt looked around the apartment in desperation. She had some options—high places were always a good bet for a cat. But Butterbean had limited choices.

The apartment didn't seem to have any hiding places that would fit a small dog.

"He's coming!" Marco yelled from the vent. "Do something! Get out!"

Walt turned to Butterbean. "Okay, we need to do a little distracting again. Operation Mini Distract. I need your nostril-licking skills."

Butterbean wagged her tail. "Sure thing!" She was always up for a good nasal probe. "This guy?" She nudged the sleeping man on the couch.

"Go for it," Walt said. If they woke the man up, there was a good chance he and the Coin Man would fight. And if they were fighting, they might not notice a smallish dog and cat slipping into the hallway.

It was a chance, anyway.

Butterbean leaned over and, with surgical precision, licked up the sleeping man's nose. He wiped at his face with his hand.

She licked again, doing the power move she liked to think of as the "brain lick."

The man swatted sleepily at his face, and his eyelids fluttered. Butterbean looked deep into his eyes and licked again. The man shrieked and staggered to his feet, scattering coins everywhere.

Butterbean nodded. "Three licks usually does it."

The key turned in the lock.

"BEAN, RUN!" Walt raced toward the front door.

Butterbean leaped off the couch and skidded down the hallway, coming to a stop behind Walt just as the door started to open.

Walt and Butterbean pressed themselves against the wall behind the door. The space was so small that the door was almost touching Butterbean's nose. She turned her head to the side and squished herself flatter.

"What is this?" The Coin Man's voice was cold.

Butterbean cringed. They'd been caught. She didn't think she'd be able to cute her way out of this one.

But nothing happened. She slowly opened one eye. The Coin Man was standing in front of the couch with a gold coin in his hand. He flipped it up into the air and caught it. Then he did it again. And he never once stopped staring at the Number Two Man, who was cringing back onto the sofa cushions and looking confused.

"I . . . don't know where this all came from. I just . . . it was just there." Number Two winced as he said it. No one would ever believe that, especially not the Coin Man.

He didn't.

"This all just appeared after you decided to 'nap'?" He flipped the coin into the air again and caught it.

"I must've been drugged?" Number Two watched the coin and swallowed hard. No one would believe that, either. Because it was ridiculous.

"Yes, of course," the Coin Man said, taking a step forward. "Drugged. By whom?"

"I don't know," Number Two said softly.

Walt nudged Butterbean hard. "Bean! Now! While we have a chance."

They stepped out carefully from behind the door. The Coin Man didn't look around. Neither did the second man.

Walt and Butterbean turned and ran down the hallway as fast as they could. When they reached the elevator, they stopped and looked back.

There was no one following them. They'd made it. They were free.

Oscar kicked the phone in frustration. He'd called the police three times. He'd double-checked the number. He'd seen it on the Television, so he knew he was doing it right. But for some reason it wasn't working the way it did on his shows.

He dialed again.

"District Eighteen Police Department, how can I help you?" The woman's voice came through the phone lying on the table.

Oscar cleared his throat. "I'd like to report a kidnapping please. The address is—"

"I'm sorry, what? I can't understand you. Speak up, please."

Oscar's feathers puffed in frustration. He spoke as clearly as he could. "I. Would. Like. To. Report. A. Kidnapping."

"This number is for police matters, not for funny voices and jokes, young man. Don't call again unless you have serious criminal activity to report." The line went dead.

Oscar stared at the phone in despair. The others were in danger, and there was nothing he could do. Operation Outside Authorities was going to fail. He couldn't get anyone to understand him, let alone believe him. And he'd been so proud of his Human language skills.

The door to the apartment opened, and Walt and Butterbean raced inside.

"We did it!" Butterbean said.

"Operation Divide and Conquer seems to be working well," Walt said, hopping up onto the desk next to Oscar. "How's Operation Outside Authorities?"

Oscar gave Walt a pained look. "A failure. They won't talk to me. They either think I'm prank calling, or they don't understand me at all."

Walt nodded sympathetically. "Humans are terrible on the phone. Let's try the software. They like talking to computers."

Walt went to the computer keyboard and typed carefully. She was a two-paw typist, but Oscar was surprised at how quick she was. She gestured toward the phone. "Could you dial for me? Call the emergency number."

Oscar nodded. "Good plan." Maybe they'd be more helpful than the police.

They slid the phone closer to the computer speaker and waited while it rang. "Nine one one, what's your emergency?"

Walt hit a key on the computer.

"I'd like to report a kidnapping," a woman's computer voice said.

"IT'S THE ELEVATOR LADY!" Butterbean gasped.

Walt frowned at her. "It's not the elevator lady."

"What is your address, please?" the 911 operator said.

Walt hit the computer button. "The Strathmore Building. The kidnappers are on the ninth floor of the Strathmore. Apartment 9B," the computer voice said.

"But, Walt!" Butterbean said, standing up to get a closer look at the computer.

"It's not her," Walt said.

Butterbean nosed at the speaker. "But . . . is it her sister?"

Walt and Oscar exchanged glances.

"Yes. It's her sister," Oscar said. He was going to need Walt to explain all of this when it was over. He didn't even know if the elevator lady had a sister.

Walt hit the button again. "The kidnappers have kidnapped a girl. She's in danger. They are also coin thieves. They have stolen coins. Please hurry."

"May I have your name, ma'am?" the 911 operator asked.

"Hang up, Oscar," Walt whispered.

"Ma'am?"

Oscar disconnected the phone.

Walt sat back on her haunches. "Operation Outside Authorities complete." She twitched an ear. "Let's just hope it works."

⭢⭠⭢⭠⭢⭠⭢⭠⭢⭠⭢⭠⭢⭠⭢⭠

Marco had promised to keep watch over what happened in the apartment. And he would keep his promise. But nobody said he couldn't cover his eyes and peek through his fingers.

At least he hadn't left his post at the grate. Wallace had retreated farther back into the vent and was sitting by the down vent, dangling his feet. It was all too intense for him.

Nothing bad had even happened yet. But that almost made it worse. Marco was sure the Coin Man was going to snap at any second, and he definitely didn't want to see what would happen to the Number Two Man then.

"Has he killed the other man yet?" Wallace yelled to Marco. He didn't want to see anything that was going on, but he didn't want to miss any of it either.

"Not yet," Marco squeaked. It was only a matter of time, though. That was obvious. That Number Two Guy was super dead.

"This is why I don't come up here, Marco!" Wallace called over his shoulder. "THIS!" He stared down the vent tube. "I don't enjoy carnage, Marco!"

"Shh," Marco said. He had to focus.

"You think you can double-cross me?" The Coin Man loomed over the other man. He was speaking so quietly that Marco had to strain to hear him. Marco shivered. Yelling would have been easier to take, somehow. "You have made a mistake, my friend. You realize that? A very big mistake."

"I understand," Number Two said. His eyes were on the floor.

"When I left an hour ago, I had one problem and no coins. Now my coins are back, and I have two problems. So you know what that means?" The Coin Man carefully put the coin he'd been flipping on the coffee table and started to roll up his sleeves.

"What?" Number Two whispered.

"Soon I will have no problems. Because I'm going to make those problems go away."

"No, please . . ." the second man whispered again. "Please."

Marco stood up. He was already going to have nightmares for a month, and he didn't see how watching this was going to help Polo. He wasn't even sure how she was going to get out. It didn't look like Walt's plan was going to work after all.

"Can you watch the living room for a minute?" Marco asked. "I want to check on Polo." Even if he couldn't help her, he could be there for moral support.

"I can't watch! You KNOW that!" Wallace said. "I never should've agreed to this." Wallace didn't know why he'd gotten mixed up with those weird apartment rats. He didn't need new friends. He had plenty of friends on the loading docks. Sure, they didn't have sunflower seeds, but who cared about that? He'd been meaning to give up sunflower seeds anyway.

Marco glared at the back of Wallace's head. He felt like punching something. "Come on, Wallace, I just need—"

With a loud crash, the door to the apartment burst open. Marco gasped.

"What? What is it?" Wallace called, twisting around to look.

"WHOOHOOO!" Marco climbed up onto the grate to get a better view. "Wallace, LOOK! It worked!"

"What worked?" Wallace hopped to his feet and took a few steps toward the grate before stopping. He didn't want to go back. But he really didn't want to miss out. "What is it?"

"It's the police!" Marco stuck his face through one of the holes in the grate and cheered. Not that anyone inside noticed him, but he thought it was appropriate anyway.

Wallace rushed to stand beside him. The apartment was crawling with police officers. The Coin Man and the Number Two Man were both handcuffed. Number Two was sobbing, with what Marco secretly suspected was relief. (Because if those police hadn't shown up, he would've been totally dead.)

Wallace pointed toward the bathroom door. "Marco, look!"

A police officer moved the chair away from the door and pushed it open. A very dazed-looking Madison stepped tentatively into the room. Two more officers rushed forward and helped her to the couch.

"Do you see her?" Marco said, craning his neck to get a better view. She had to be okay. "Can you see Polo?"

"There!" Wallace pointed again. "Look at the pocket!"

Polo's head had popped up out of Madison's pocket. She was grinning from ear to ear, and when she saw Marco and Wallace in the grate, she gave them a thumbs-up.

Marco gave her a thumbs-up too, then leaned down to put his head between his knees. He needed to take some deep, cleansing breaths.

"I'd get you a paper bag to breathe into," Wallace said. "But it would be too big."

"I'll be okay," Marco said. "I just need a minute."

Wallace patted him on the back. "I understand. Hey, what's Polo doing?"

Marco stood up and looked into the room again. Polo was hanging out of the jacket pocket and clutching the material of Madison's sweater.

Madison didn't notice, and neither did the police officer taking her statement.

In just a few seconds, Polo withdrew back into the pocket. Looking up at the vent grate, she held up her hand triumphantly.

She had a new button.

– 19 –

"WE DID IT! IT WORKED!" MARCO RACED OUT FROM the vent behind the couch. "The police arrested them and everything."

"Is Polo okay?" Butterbean asked, rushing up to sniff him. He smelled pretty much like he usually did, but she liked to check, just in case.

Marco raised his arms to give Butterbean full sniff access. "She looked fine. Wallace said he'd keep watching. She'll probably be back soon." Marco pumped his fist. "WHOOHOO!"

"Whew! Finally some good news." Walt hopped off the window ledge, where she'd been sitting with

Oscar. "We've been watching the police cars drive up. I'm glad they got there in time."

"Wow, two successful heists in one day!" Butterbean said, sitting down and scratching her ear. "We're awesome!"

"We're the best heisters ever!" Marco cheered.

"And now we're poor!" Butterbean cheered.

"Yes, about that—" Oscar started, hopping down from the ledge.

"About that," Walt said, cutting him off. "I'm not going to a shelter. I'm a black cat, and black cats don't do well at shelters. The whole 'unlucky' thing." She attempted to make air quotes, without much success. "So when Bob comes to get us, I'm planning to slip out. I can take care of myself. I'd appreciate it if you don't draw attention to it."

Butterbean looked horrified. "No! Walt, we'll figure something out!" Butterbean raced over to Oscar. "We need to stay together! Right, Oscar? We'll make a new plan!"

"Wallace invited me and Polo to live in the vents. I'm sure he wouldn't mind if the rest of you came. It's an option," Marco said. Then he caught sight of Butterbean's stricken face. "Well, not for Butterbean. Sorry about that." Marco wrung his hands apologetically. "But you're cute—you're sure to get adopted quickly."

"Or maybe the power walker woman can take you!" Walt said encouragingly. "She seems nice."

"No! You can't live in the vents without me!" Butterbean whimpered.

"Listen, about that—" Oscar started again.

"Are you going to come live in the vents, Oscar?" Marco said.

"Um, no." Oscar shuddered. "If it came down to it, I'd head to the park. I hear there are some lovely trees there. But listen—"

"No! No trees, no vents, no slipping out! We've got to stick together!" Butterbean turned to Oscar, her eyes moist. "We just need a new plan, right, Oscar? Can't you think of something? You've got all the best plans."

Walt bumped her head up against Butterbean's side. "Butterbean, think about it," she said. "Giving the money back was the right thing to do, but now that we aren't independently wealthy, we can't live on our own. And besides, we don't even have anyone to take care of us."

"We've got Madison," Butterbean said stubbornly.

"We don't have Madison. Not anymore," Marco said. "She's living alone, remember, no adult? Those cops have to know that by now. Do you think they're going to let her keep doing that?"

Butterbean tried to be positive. "Maybe?"

"No chance," Walt said, frowning. "She'll be sent to what, an orphanage?"

"I don't think they do orphanages that much anymore," Oscar said. He wasn't sure, though. There were lots of orphanages on the Television, but Oscar was starting to doubt how accurate his shows really were.

Marco rolled his eyes. "Well, wherever she goes, it won't be here. She won't be feeding us," he said.

"Marco is right, Butterbean," Walt said sympathetically. "I wish we had options. But we now have zero people to take care of us. Bob is coming. Face it, our time is up."

Butterbean opened her mouth to protest, but just then a key turned in the lock.

"Bob!" Marco gasped, racing for his aquarium. "No, it's too soon!" Polo wasn't even back yet. Marco gritted his teeth. He wasn't going anywhere without Polo. Not without a fight.

The door opened, and Butterbean screamed in delight.

It was Mrs. Food.

She was sitting in a chair wheeled by Bob, who positioned Mrs. Food next to the couch.

"MRS. FOOD!" Butterbean shrieked, racing to the chair and jumping up in an attempt to climb into Mrs. Food's lap and lick her nostrils all at the same time.

Bob did not look amused. "Yeah, back in the apartment, huh? I'm onto you, dog," he muttered, pushing Butterbean away from Mrs. Food. He turned and glared at Walt. "Don't think I didn't see you, too, cat."

Mrs. Food laughed weakly and reached down to scratch Butterbean behind the ears. "Calm down, Bean," she said.

Butterbean sat down, wagging her tail so hard that she looked like she was going to levitate. Bob shifted uncomfortably. "Now, do you need me to get your stuff together, or . . ."

Mrs. Food half turned to look at him. "I think I can manage. I can get out of the chair myself. You don't have to stay."

Bob looked relieved. "Well, good. That lady, your what, Elder Care lady? She'll be here soon, so she can help with anything you can't do. Sorry to see you go, ma'am."

"Me too, Bob." Mrs. Food looked sad.

She sat absentmindedly patting Butterbean's head until she heard Bob leave. Then she turned back to the animals. "Now, all of you, stay calm. I have some bad news."

Walt hopped up onto the arm of the wheelchair. Oscar flew over to the coffee table. Marco perched on top of his water bottle. Then they waited. This was it. It was finally happening.

Mrs. Food folded her hands in her lap. "I know this has all been very scary for you. And I wish I had better news. I'm well now, but the doctors said I'm not well enough to live on my own. And I can't take you with me to the care facility I'm going to. So you're all going to have to go to new homes."

"Shelter," Walt said softly.

Butterbean gave a low wail.

Mrs. Food sighed. "I'll do my best to find places for you. I've already started asking around. I'm so sorry." She rubbed Butterbean's ear. Butterbean's leg started to thump. "The nurse is going to be up in just a minute to help me get my things, but I wanted to let you know myself."

Butterbean launched herself up at Mrs. Food's face again. She looked so sad. Butterbean couldn't stand it.

Loud footsteps echoed in the hallway.

Mrs. Food sighed. "Bob again," she said, reaching out and stroking Walt's neck. "I wish we had more time."

The door burst open so violently that it banged against the opposite wall. A small figure raced in, slamming the door again behind her. It was a very un-Bob-like way to open a door. That was probably because it wasn't Bob. It was Madison.

She was clutching Polo in a sweaty grip and stopped short when she saw Mrs. Food. "Oh. Mrs. Fudeker. I'm really sorry. I didn't know you were . . . I just . . . Is this your rat?"

Mrs. Food reached out for Polo. "Why yes, Polo! How nice of you to return her." Polo crawled into Mrs. Food's hand and hugged one of her fingers.

Madison glanced back toward the door. "Yeah, they said I wasn't supposed to, but I had to, right? I mean, she's your rat." She reached down and patted Butterbean on the head. "I've been taking care of these guys while you've been gone, but I can't anymore. They're taking me—" She broke off in a strangled sob. "Anyway, I wanted to say thank you? To these guys, and to you, I guess." She looked around the room at the animals. "I don't know how you did it. But I know it was you. So thank you." She looked at Mrs. Food again. "They'll understand."

Mrs. Food nodded. "I'm sure they will." She hesitated. "You're Ruby Park's niece?"

More footsteps could be heard in the hallway. Madison winced at the sound. "Yeah. Anyway, sorry about barging in. I just—"

The door flew open, and a tall red-faced woman

in a blazer stood in the doorway. "Madison! I told you we were going straight to the car." She turned to Mrs. Food. "I'm sorry to disturb you, ma'am. I'm Mrs. Taylor, and this little girl is on her way to her new foster home. I'm sure you heard about the incident on the top floor? We'll just be leaving now." She gripped Madison by the upper arm and pulled her toward the door.

Butterbean wuffled softly and turned her most soulful gaze toward Mrs. Food. Walt bumped her head against Mrs. Food's arm, purr volume turned up to high. Even Polo blinked in her cutest way (although she was severely hampered by her sweaty, matted fur).

Mrs. Food gave the slightest nod and put on a puzzled expression. "But why?"

Mrs. Taylor hesitated. "Why what, ma'am?"

"Why are you taking her to a foster home? She already has a home. She lives here, with me," Mrs. Food said, frowning.

"What? What do you mean?" Mrs. Taylor glanced from Mrs. Food to Madison and back again.

"I mean she lives here. Why? What were you told?" Mrs. Food's voice was chilly.

"Wait, you mean . . . I'm sorry. She lives here?" Mrs. Taylor looked at Madison accusingly. "She didn't say she lives here. No one told me she had a guardian."

Mrs. Food sniffed. "Well, I can't help that. It was all arranged with her aunt, Ruby Park. Madison is staying here with me while her aunt is deployed in . . . Where is it again, dear?"

"Afghanistan," Madison said, hardly daring to breathe.

"Afghanistan, yes," Mrs. Food said. "You can check with her if you like, but we have it all arranged. It's very convenient, you see, because we live in the same building."

"That's what I meant when I said I lived downstairs," Madison said, shooting a hopeful look at Mrs. Food. "I didn't mean my aunt's apartment on the eighth floor—I meant here. I tried to tell you."

Mrs. Taylor glared at them both suspiciously. Mrs. Food and Madison stared back without even blinking, they were trying so hard to look innocent.

Mrs. Taylor reluctantly let go of Madison's arm. "Oh. Well. I will be checking on this, I can tell you that," she huffed. "But if your aunt set it up . . ."

"She did. It's in my Family Care Plan," Madison said. "That's why it was so important for me to come here. So Mrs. Fudeker could explain."

"Well. I see. Well," Mrs. Taylor fumed. "Thank you for your help then, Mrs. Fudeker. We'll be in touch."

"Thank you," Mrs. Food said calmly. Mrs. Taylor turned stiffly and marched out.

Madison whipped around to face Mrs. Food. "This isn't going to work, is it? They'll never fall for it! We'll get in trouble. They'll check and see it's not true!"

Mrs. Food smiled. "It won't matter if they check if we fix things first. Listen, Madison, would you like to live here with me while your aunt is away? We can call Mrs. Taylor back if you don't want to."

"I definitely want to!"

"Good. I'd love to have you here. And I'm not supposed to live alone right now either, so it's good for both of us. Now, what do we have to do to get in touch with your aunt—can you call her?" Mrs. Food stood up carefully. "There's a phone in the office."

"I can e-mail her," Madison said quickly. "She's always liked you, so she'll definitely say yes. I think she just needs to change the plan she filed for me."

"Then e-mail, quickly. The computer's in the office too. And then go get your things—we'll get you set up in the guest bedroom."

Madison grinned. "Got it."

Mrs. Food smiled tightly. "Now the only problem is my nurse. She should be here any—"

"Mrs. Fudeker?" A small woman slipped in the front door and almost bumped into Madison. The woman jumped back in surprise. "Oh! I'm sorry, but . . ." She looked at Madison in confusion. "Who is this? Mrs. Fudeker? I understood you lived alone?"

Mrs. Food raised her eyebrows significantly at Madison. "Sheila, this is—"

Madison leaped forward, hand extended. "I'm Madison Park. I live here. With Mrs. Fudeker." She shook Sheila's hand enthusiastically.

"You live here! But . . ." The woman frowned and looked at her clipboard.

"It's all set up in my Family Care Plan," Madison said, a huge smile plastered on her face. "I'm living here while my aunt is deployed."

"That's true," Mrs. Food confirmed.

The small woman nodded and flipped through the papers. "But Mrs. Fudeker, all your paperwork says you live alone."

"Nope! Not alone. With me," Madison said brightly. "It's all set up."

Mrs. Food made a face. "I've been telling people all along I didn't need placement in assisted living. Not with Madison as my caregiver."

"I'm very helpful," Madison said, standing up straighter.

Sheila smiled. "I'm sure you are, hon." She flipped one last page, then threw up her hands and smiled at

Madison. "Well, it's obvious someone got something very wrong. I apologize. I'll go back to the hospital and get this cleared up." She rolled her eyes. "Clerical errors."

"That's fine." Mrs. Food smiled. "And thank you."

"Yeah, thanks!" Madison said, waving goodbye until the woman was gone. "She bought it!"

Mrs. Food let out a sigh of relief. "E-mail, NOW!" she said, pointing to the office.

"Right!" Madison turned and raced inside.

A few minutes later she stuck her head out. "Mrs. Fudeker, did you call in a tip to the crime line? There's a message saying something about a reward."

– 20 –

Don't get me wrong—I'll gladly accept the reward if they give it to me," Mrs. Food said as she put a sandwich and pretzels into Madison's lunch bag. "But what I don't understand is HOW? I wasn't even home when that call was made."

"Beats me, but don't tell them that!" Madison said, stashing her lunch in her book bag. "It's really weird, though."

"Belly rub," Butterbean said, rolling over onto her back at Madison's feet.

"Weird and lucky." Madison reached down to scratch Butterbean's tummy. "Maybe you've got a guardian angel."

Butterbean caught Walt's eye and winked. Walt winked back. Mrs. Food and Madison didn't suspect a thing.

Madison frowned. She stopped scratching and looked from Butterbean to Walt thoughtfully. Butterbean lolled her tongue out of her mouth and drooled a little. It never hurt to look a tiny bit stupid.

"Maybe more than one," Madison said, winking at Butterbean. Butterbean almost choked on her spit. Smirking, Walt jumped off the chair and stalked into the living room. Well, at least Mrs. Food didn't suspect anything.

"Now, don't forget your call with your aunt after school today," Mrs. Food said.

"Got it." Madison patted Butterbean goodbye. "See you later!" She threw her bag over her shoulder and hurried out.

Madison's aunt had agreed to the new living arrangement right away and was horrified that Madison had been living on her own for so long. Mrs. Food was officially Madison's guardian for as long as her aunt was deployed. Walt and Oscar had hoped to be named guardians too and were more than a little offended that no one had even asked them.

Mrs. Food wiped her hands on a dish towel and made her way down the hallway to her office, carefully checking for any obstacles placed in her path. The last thing she wanted was a return trip to the hospital. But she didn't need to worry. Butterbean had a new policy—from now on, whenever she barfed, she would immediately clean it up herself. So far it seemed to be working well.

"I still don't see why SHE gets the reward," Butterbean grumbled, grabbing her squeaky carrot and tossing it into the air after Mrs. Food had closed the office door. "I mean, it was Walt and Oscar who called. And the elevator lady's sister. THEY should get the reward."

"It'll be easier for her to spend it," Walt said wearily. They'd had this conversation at least five times. "And think of it this way—we got two caretakers out of the deal. Now if something goes wrong with Mrs. Food again, we have a backup."

"But we had a treasure! And now we're poor!" There was just something about those gold coins. Butterbean really would've liked to roll in them one last time.

"Polo got a new button," Marco pointed out. Mrs. Food had left the rats' aquarium out in the living room—the other animals had objected when she tried to move it back to the office. And Marco and Polo were enjoying their new view.

"That's right. That's kind of like a treasure," Polo

said, admiring the button around her neck. Marco had tied the string in a double knot this time.

"I guess so," Butterbean said, sitting up.

A cabinet door slammed. "What the heck?" Oscar craned his neck to look into the kitchen. "That's not Chad again, is it?"

"Hey, Chad," Butterbean said. It was Chad. Again.

Chad was sitting in the sink with a package of sardines he'd gotten from the cabinet. He grabbed the pull tab with one of his tentacles and sucked the sardines down without a word. So far Mrs. Food hadn't

noticed how quickly they'd been disappearing.

"You know, one day Mrs. Food is going to catch you doing that and it'll all be over," Walt said, licking a paw. "She's cool, but I don't know if she's strange-octopus-in-the-sink cool."

"Hey, guys!" Wallace emerged from behind the sofa. His cheeks were filled with sunflower seeds, and he was leaving a trail of shells as he walked.

"Is she strange-rat-in-the-living-room cool?" Butterbean asked.

"She's going to have to be. After all, they're members of our gang. Go, Strathmore Six!" Marco cheered.

"Marco!" Polo hissed. "Rude! Wallace isn't a member. It's the Strathmore SIX, get it? He'd make it seven."

Wallace stopped chewing and looked at them, hurt. A shell dropped out of his mouth. "You guys have a gang?"

"More of an International Crime Syndicate," Oscar said. He hopped onto the Television and snapped his beak. "All in favor of including Wallace and making it the Strathmore Seven?"

"WHOOOHOO!" Marco cheered, high-fiving Wallace, who choked on a seed.

"Sounds good to me," Walt said.

"Me too!" Butterbean yelped. "Strathmore Seven!"

"Any more sardines?" Chad asked.

"I've never been in a club. Thanks, you guys." Wallace blushed. "But I wanted to tell you—the Patchouli Family was watching the news. The heist is on TV. Channel Seven."

"Ooh, we're famous!" Oscar crowed, hopping on the remote and turning the Television to Channel Seven.

". . . Prosecutors say that an anonymous tip led police to the apartment, where they were able to arrest the thieves and recover most of the coins that had been stolen."

"Wait a minute." Walt stepped on the pause button. "MOST of the coins?"

Oscar shifted from foot to foot. "Hmm. Wow. That's, um. Interesting."

Walt cocked her head. "Oscar?"

Oscar sighed. "FINE." He hopped over to the sofa and dragged Mrs. Food's embroidered bag out from underneath. With obvious effort, he tossed it into the middle of the living room.

The flap burst open, and gold coins spilled out.

Five jaws dropped simultaneously.

Oscar folded his wings. "Well, you didn't expect me to return ALL of them, did you?" he grumbled. "What if it happens again? We might NEED them!"

Walt flopped back onto her haunches. "Well, that's it. We're officially criminals."

"But criminals who can do this!" Butterbean yelped, bouncing in excitement. "Oscar, can I?"

Oscar swept his wing in the direction of the coins. "Feel free." He looked at Marco and Polo and Wallace. "You too." He winked at Marco. "Now's the appropriate time."

"WHOOHOO!" Marco shrieked, pumping his fists.

With cheers of happiness, Butterbean, Marco, Polo, and Wallace all threw themselves into the small pile of coins, rolling around and flinging coins in the air.

Walt and Oscar exchanged glances.

"Oh, heck," Walt said, jumping in after them. Oscar was only a second behind her.

And across the room, Chad began inching toward the celebration. He was an expert coin flinger.

Acknowledgments

This book would not have been possible without the hard work of the amazing people at Atheneum. I was so lucky to get to work with you all.

Special thanks to Reka Simonsen (rock star), Kate Testerman (also a rock star), and David Mottram (another rock star) for bringing Butterbean and the rest of the Strathmore Seven to life.

Thanks also to:

The real life Colleen and Elizabeth, for being such good sports and letting me borrow your names.

The real life Bob, whose name I also borrowed, and who was one of my dog Binky's favorite people.

My SCBWI friends, for encouraging me even when I got stuck halfway through the book.

My family, for reading endless revisions without complaint (to me, anyway) and for helping me look for the flash drive containing the first *Pet Heist* draft long after it was obvious that it had disappeared forever. (If anyone ever finds it, let me know.)

And finally, thanks to the elevator voice at the Hyatt Regency Century Plaza. The way you say "lobby" gets me every time.

(No animals were harmed in the making of this book. However, some did have their schedules rearranged, their meals delayed, and their walks cut short. Apologies to all.)

Turn the page for a sneak peek at
THE GREAT GHOST HOAX

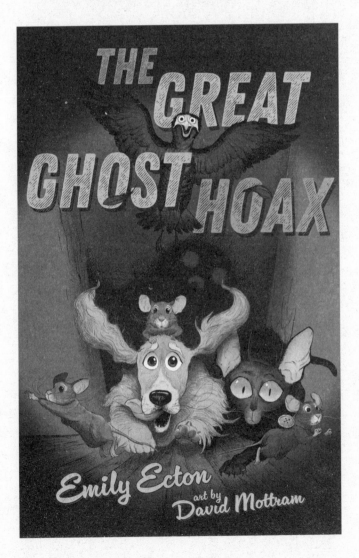

THE GREAT GHOST HOAX

Emily Ecton

art by David Mottram

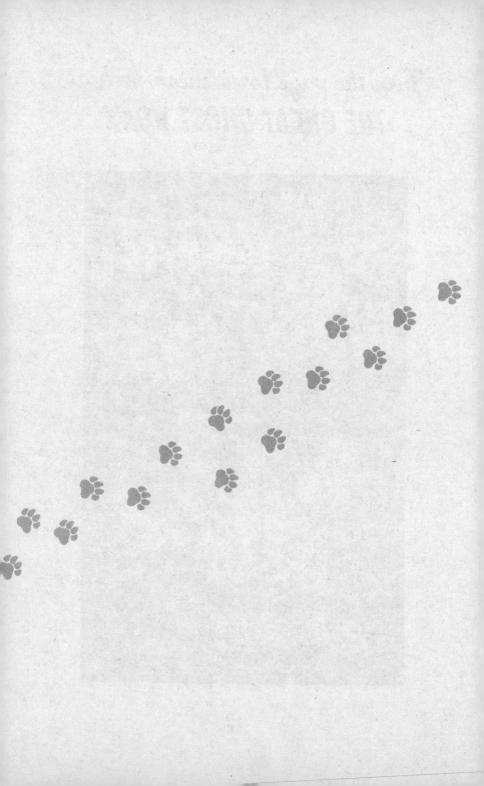

"NOTHING EXCITING EVER HAPPENS TO US!" Butterbean wailed, flopping over onto her back in the living room. She'd hoped that saying that would make something exciting magically happen, but it didn't work.

She'd done her best to make the day fun. She'd finished chewing her rawhide chew. She'd disemboweled her squeaky lamb toy and carefully scattered its stuffing around the living room. She'd attempted to tunnel through the living room carpet (unsuccessfully). There was nothing left to do. She'd done it all.

"Nothing! Nothing exciting ever happens!" Butterbean wailed again, in a different key this time. She liked to mix things up.

Walt rolled her eyes and inspected her paw. "Hello, remember heisting?"

"I wouldn't call an International Crime Syndicate nothing," Oscar sniffed, puffing out his feathers indignantly. He wasn't about to let Butterbean diminish his status as an International Crime Boss. Not to mention the fact that he was the only crime boss who was also a mynah bird. It was no small feat.

Butterbean rolled over onto her stomach. "That was a million years ago. Nothing happens NOW. Just look! Everything's BORING. And even Madison is gone!" Madison was the medium-sized girl who had moved in with them temporarily while her aunt was deployed overseas.

"Madison is at school," Oscar said, absentmindedly flipping through one of Mrs. Food's magazines. "She goes to school every day, Butterbean. It's a thing humans do."

"Not the other day," Butterbean whined. "It wasn't school the other day."

Walt sighed. "We've gone over this, Bean. That was a field trip, and she came back! She always comes back!" Walt shook her head. "You need to get a grip."

"A FIELD TRIP." Butterbean pouted. "WITHOUT US."

"Let it go, Butterbean," Oscar said, hopping on the

remote to unmute the Television. "The News is back on. They're about to identify the common household appliance that can make us go bald."

Ever since their heist, Oscar had been obsessed with the News. Butterbean wasn't even sure why. It wasn't like the News was even talking about their heist anymore. They were old news. On the other hand, she didn't want to go bald.

Butterbean blew on a piece of squeaky-lamb fluff and groaned.

"I get it, Butterbean," Marco said, climbing out of his cage and plunking down next to her. "Us former criminal types have a hard time adjusting to regular life. It's rough. But at least you see Madison. I barely ever see Wallace anymore."

"SEE? Wallace is GONE," Butterbean said triumphantly, sitting up.

"Shhhh," Oscar hissed, turning the volume up on the Television. "Bald, Butterbean."

Walt finished licking her paw. "Moving into a new apartment isn't gone. Wallace just got his own place."

"It's not like he lived with us anyway," Polo said, following Marco's lead and climbing out of their cage. "Wallace is still a wild rat, you know."

Wallace was a former pet rat who lived in the Strathmore Building's seventh-floor vents. But a few weeks ago he'd discovered an empty apartment on the fifth floor. And since nobody seemed to be using it, he'd moved his stuff in and sent out change-of-address notices. (Polo thought that was a little formal, but Wallace seemed very proud.)

"Nothing wrong with a little peace and quiet," Walt said, examining her other paw.

"Personally, I like retirement. It's relaxing! We've got Mrs. Food, and how many people have an extra bonus person to take care of them? We've got it made!" Marco patted Butterbean on the paw.

"And it's not like nothing exciting will ever happen again," Polo said, patting the other paw. "Something exciting could happen AT ANY TIME!"

"Right! Something could happen right now!" Marco chimed in.

Polo nodded. "Or now!"

Marco tilted his head and waited a second. "Or now!"

Polo grinned. "Right. Or now!"

"Cut it out, you guys," Walt said.

"Or not," Polo said. "Maybe not RIGHT now."

Walt sighed. "Bean, we can't expect something exciting to happen just because we're bored."

"AHA! So you're bored too!" Butterbean jumped to her feet. "I knew it!" she barked happily. "You—"

But she never finished the sentence. Because that's when the pounding started.

Five heads swiveled to look at the front door. The pounding was so loud that they could almost see it— it felt like the door was bouncing inward with each blow. And with each blow the animals cringed and retreated farther into the room.

"Places, everyone!" Oscar screeched, and the animals scrambled so they wouldn't be caught out of their cages. Oscar had barely gotten his cage door closed before Mrs. Food appeared in the hallway, carefully making her way toward the front door. (She was always extra careful now, ever since she'd slipped in a patch of Butterbean's barf and had to go to the hospital. Nobody wanted that to happen again, especially Butterbean. She still felt guilty.)

"Don't open it!" Butterbean yelped. She could feel the hairs on her back prickling. She didn't want to know what was outside in that hallway. Trying to get in.

But Mrs. Food didn't listen.

Taking a deep breath, Mrs. Food threw the door open. In one swift motion, the thing in the hallway lunged at Mrs. Food, clutching her and sobbing into her shoulder.

"AAAAHHH!" Polo shrieked, diving underneath the cedar bedding in the corner of the cage.

"URGH!" Mrs. Food braced herself against the door frame as the thing squeezed her. It was shaking and making weird squeaky hiccuppy noises.

Walt crouched down, flexing her claws. "I'll go for the eyes!" Going for the eyes was Walt's go-to attack method.

"Wait, is that . . ." Butterbean sniffed. The monster attacking Mrs. Food smelled very familiar. And it kind of looked more like a hug-attack than an attack-attack. And what kind of monster made squeaky sobs?

"Wait, who . . ." Oscar craned his neck to get a better look.

Butterbean took one last sniff. "It's Mrs. Third Floor!" she gasped.

"Stand down, Walt." Oscar snapped his beak shut. Mrs. Third Floor was not an enemy.

Walt shot him a look in response, but she stayed in attack position. You could never be too sure.

Mrs. Third Floor was a lady from the building, and up until that moment, Butterbean would've said she knew everything about her. After all, she'd seen her around the building since she was a puppy. (Butterbean, not Mrs. Third Floor.)

Mrs. Third Floor lived on the third floor. She wore sturdy leather shoes. She smelled like furniture polish, arthritis cream, and peppermint. She had a scary folding wheely cart that she sometimes took outside. She always spoke to Mrs. Food and patted Butterbean on the head when she saw her. That was pretty much everything there was to know, as far as Butterbean was concerned. But Mrs. Third Floor wasn't a door pounder. And Butterbean had never ever heard her make squeaky noises like that before. She never would've guessed it was possible. Something was very wrong.

Mrs. Food looked as shocked as Butterbean felt. "What is it? What's happened?" Mrs. Food gasped. (Mrs. Third Floor was squeezing her a little too tightly.)

"It's—" Mrs. Third Floor said in a strangled voice. The entire room waited while she choked back a sob. "It's . . ." she said again. "I've had a shock," she finished apologetically.

Mrs. Food nodded. "Here. Sit." She led Mrs. Third Floor toward the sofa and helped her sit down, brushing bits of lamb fluff off the seat.

Butterbean watched with satisfaction. She'd done a very good job distributing the fluff.

"Do you want to talk about it?" Mrs. Food picked up the remote. "I'm sorry about this noise. I don't know how it got turned up so loud."

"No, keep it on—oh darn, we missed that segment on appliances," Mrs. Third Floor sniffled.

Oscar snapped his beak in irritation. He was going to go bald now, he just knew it.

"Mildred." Mrs. Food looked serious. "I don't want to talk about appliances."

"And I don't think I like that anchorwoman's dress. It's not a flattering color." Mrs. Third Floor kept her eyes locked on the Television.

"Mildred . . ."

"Oh and look! Breaking news!" Mrs. Third Floor turned to Mrs. Food with a tight smile on her face. "It's about that octopus at the zoo. Oh no, Mr. Wiggles is missing. That's terrible!"

Mrs. Food turned the Television off. Mrs. Third Floor sagged.

Oscar fluffed his feathers grouchily. First the bald thing, and now this. He was a big fan of Mr. Wiggles. He liked to keep up with all the Wiggles-related news. He just hoped Mrs. Third Floor had a good excuse for the way she was acting.

Mrs. Food patted Mrs. Third Floor on the shoulder. "Mildred, tell me. It's okay. Whatever it is."

Mrs. Third Floor twisted her hands in her lap. "You'll think I'm being silly."

"I won't think you're being silly," Mrs. Food promised.

"Okay." Mrs. Third Floor took a deep breath. "It's

that apartment. It's haunted." She burst out in a new round of sobs.

Walt shrugged. "I think she's being silly."

"Huh." Butterbean sat back on her haunches. That hadn't been what she'd expected. "Haunted?"

"I was going to guess a natural disaster," Oscar said. "Although they probably would've covered that on the News. IF WE'D SEEN IT."

"It's just your basic nervous breakdown," Walt said, getting up and stretching. "Nothing to see here."

Mrs. Food had a strange expression on her face. It didn't look like a haunted apartment was what she'd expected either. "Haunted? You mean haunted haunted? As in, um . . . ghosts?"

"WAIT, WHAT?" Butterbean yelped. "GHOSTS?"

"She's losing it, Bean," Walt sighed. "There aren't ghosts."

"Yes, GHOSTS," Mrs. Third Floor wailed. "There are GHOSTS in my beautiful rental unit. What am I going to do?"

Mrs. Food scanned the room, like she was going to find the answer lying around somewhere. Like in a book called *Ghosts: How to Handle Them* or *What to Do If Your Friend Flips Out*. "I'm sure there's a reasonable explanation," she said finally.

"THERE IS NO REASONABLE EXPLA-NATION," Mrs. Third Floor screeched. Her voice was starting to hurt Butterbean's ears, it was that shrill.

"Okay, so explain," Mrs. Food said. "How do you know you have ghosts?"

Mrs. Third Floor took a deep breath. "You know I've been getting that furnished apartment on five ready for renters? Well, for the past few days, there have been SIGNS. Of SUPERNATURAL ACTIVITY." She sat back on the cushions, crossing her arms as if there was no need for further discussion.

Mrs. Food frowned. "Signs?"

"PARANORMAL SIGNS," Mrs. Third Floor snapped. Her jaw was set.

Walt snorted. "Please. As if."

Mrs. Food nodded slowly. "Right. Supernatural activity. Paranormal signs. Of course. Let me get you some tea." She stood up abruptly and hurried over to the kitchen.

Oscar's eyes narrowed. "Wait, five? Did she say the apartment on five?"

Butterbean knew this one. "She did. She said there are GHOSTS. On FIVE."

Walt shot Oscar a look. "Oh no," she groaned.

"Yep." Oscar sighed.

"What?" Butterbean looked from Walt to Oscar in confusion. She hated it when they had secrets.

"Oh, I know!" Marco piped up from the rat aquarium. "Isn't that where Wallace lives now?"

Walt made a face. "Exactly."

"WHAT?" Butterbean gasped. "WALLACE IS A GHOST?"

"No, Bean. Wallace isn't a ghost. But it's got to be him. Whatever he's been doing is freaking Mrs. Third Floor out. That's the obvious explanation," Oscar said, shaking his head sadly.

"Right. Okay." Butterbean didn't know why Wallace would do something like that, but Oscar usually was right about things. Especially obvious things.

"I don't know," Polo said, fiddling with the button she wore on a string around her neck. "That doesn't sound like Wallace. He's usually pretty careful."

"I know, Polo, but this time—" Walt started, but she never finished the sentence. Because that's when they heard the screaming.

"WHAT IS HAPPENING?" Butterbean barked in alarm. She'd wanted things to get more exciting, but she hadn't counted on there being so much noise.

The screaming was echoing through the vents, and it was so loud that they were sure that even Mrs. Food must hear it.

Five heads swiveled toward the secret vent opening behind the sofa. A few seconds later a small rat came streaking out into the room.

Wallace's eyes were huge. As soon as he saw Walt, he shot over and grabbed her by the leg. "Help! Oh Walt, guys, help!" Wallace gasped.

Butterbean frowned. Polo was right. Wallace was usually a very careful rat. And right now he was being anything but careful.

Walt patted Wallace on the back as she turned her body slightly to hide him from view. Whatever was wrong, it had to be bad if he'd turned to a cat for help. And if he wasn't worried about being seen by the humans, it had to be even worse. "What is it, Wallace?" she said softly.

Wallace looked up at her and took a deep shuddering breath. "It's my apartment! On five! Guys, that apartment is HAUNTED."

Looking for another great book?
Find it
IN THE MIDDLE.

Fun, fantastic books for kids
in the in-be**TWEEN** age.

IntheMiddleBooks.com